# CAPTURED BY

*Doms of Destiny, Colorado 1*

## Chloe Lang

**MENAGE EVERLASTING**

**Siren Publishing, Inc.**
**www.SirenPublishing.com**

**A SIREN PUBLISHING BOOK**
IMPRINT: Ménage Everlasting

CAPTURED BY COWBOYS


ISBN: 978-1-62740-057-2

First Printing: May 2013

Cover design by Les Byerley


Printed in the U.S.A.

**PUBLISHER**
Siren Publishing, Inc.
www.SirenPublishing.com

# DEDICATION

Doms of Destiny, Colorado began as a discussion between me and my dear friend and sister in heart, Sophie Oak. I had already wrapped up the Strong Brothers books and was working on the next Wilde, Nevada story at the time. I mentioned to Sophie that I was thinking about starting a new series about a town of Doms. You have to know Sophie. When the wheels of her brain start whirring, she's much like a mad scientist—brilliant and dangerous. I love it. In less than an hour, we'd worked out the major details of Destiny, Colorado.

*Sophie, thank you for your never-faltering friendship and support.*

Doms of Destiny soon became my passion. I would wake up in the middle of the night as my imagination began to populate the town. More and more people showed up. My sanity was another wonderful friend—Chloe Vale. Like a midwife, doctor, therapist, Domme at times, she listened to my blathering on and on about Destiny. She's my much-needed grammarian, my sweet cheerleader, and my ever-ready listener when Destiny seems to be screaming inside me.

*Chloe, thank you. This book has your fingerprints all over it.*

Two lovely women who read for me on this book and added wonderful insight and awesome critiques were Liz Berry and Lana McLemore.

*Liz and Lana, what can I say? Thank you for being there for me on this one, and thank you for your unshakeable love and support.*

There are three people at Siren-BookStrand I want to thank, also: Diana, Courtney, and Les.

*Thank you for everything that went into this book—support, hard work, and creativity.*

Lastly, I want to thank you, the reader. Without you all of the above would be for nothing. All of us do our best to give you a place and people to fall in love with. My hope is we've done our job.

*Thank you for visiting Destiny.*

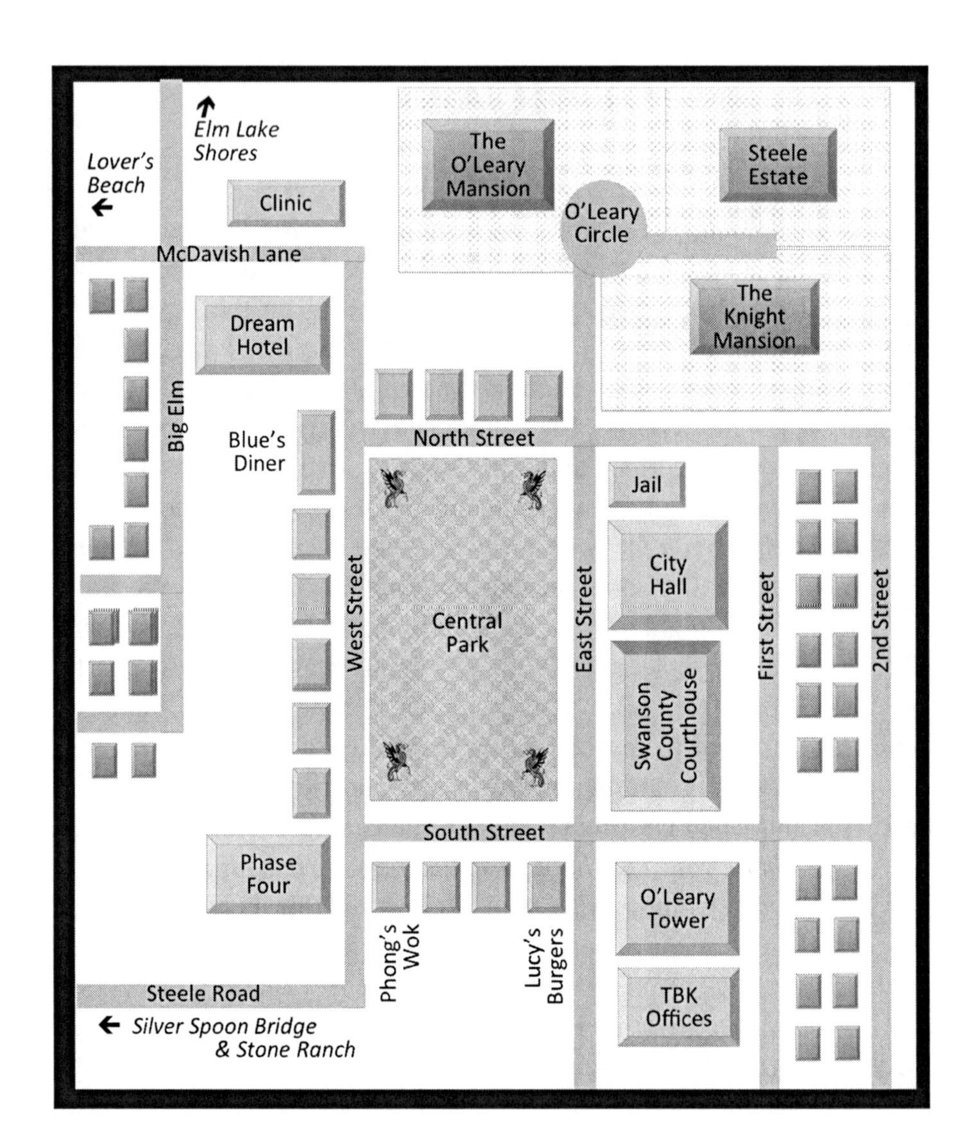
Elm Lake
Shores
Lover's
Beach
Clinic
The
O'Leary
Mansion
Steele
Estate
O'Leary
Circle
McDavish Lane
The
Knight
Mansion
Dream
Hotel
Big Elm
Blue's
Diner
North Street
Jail
City
Hall
Central
Park
West Street
East Street
First Street
2nd Street
Swanson
County
Courthouse
South Street
Phase
Four
O'Leary
Tower
Phong's
Wok
Lucy's
Burgers
TBK
Offices
Steele Road
Silver Spoon Bridge
& Stone Ranch

# CAPTURED BY COWBOYS

***Doms of Destiny, Colorado 1***

**CHLOE LANG**



## Chapter One

Emmett Stone watched the clouds darken behind and above snow-capped Blue Arrow Peak. The white flakes shouldn't be falling at this elevation until late September, another four months from now, but by the feel and smell of the air and the look of the sky, he knew their raindrop cousins were about to come down in buckets. "We better get back to the cabin and pronto, buddy." He patted his horse's thick neck.

Bullet, his constant companion for the past thirteen years, snorted his agreement. The steed still had some life left in him, thank God, though his gait had been slowed by time. Galloping was unfortunately relegated to bygone years for his four-legged, chestnut-colored friend.

Emmett got up in the old boy's saddle in a single bound. The wind was picking up speed at his back, fueling the coming storm. It was definitely going to be one helluva squall.

Warning his younger brothers, who were working the south part of the ranch, would've been best. Too bad cell service didn't work up here. The roads, all of them dirt for miles and miles, would likely wash out, making travel by horseback rough, and by truck, which Cody and Bryant were in, impossible. Their ranch hands, Sawyer and Reed Coleman, were safe in town at their sister's for her birthday.

He looked at his watch and thought that his brothers might make it back to the cabin in time if they cut out a little early, though he doubted they would. Like him, they put in a good ten to twelve hours each and every day.

Ranch life could be hard, but it also had its rewards, which were many. Those rewards had kept him and his brothers in line since they were kids. They'd kept the ranch and built it into something to be very proud of. According to the accountants, their assets—the land, livestock, and other holdings—were worth well into the hundreds of millions of dollars. He should've been satisfied with the success, but he wasn't. The all-too-familiar gnawing at the back of his mind inched up into his consciousness, making him feel unsettled and restless. He shifted in the saddle and tried to shove the nagging thoughts away. It didn't work. The longing had grown and grown over the past few years. Why? He wasn't even sure what it was he was longing for.

"Bullet, I need to be more like you. Take things one day at a time. Thinking too much gets a man in trouble." He tugged on the reins slightly, guiding his horse through the gate and onto the county road that edged the ranch. He dismounted and closed the gate. Turning back to Bullet, he spotted something about a quarter mile up the road. Was it a downed animal?

He jumped on the horse and headed that direction, the opposite way of the cabin. Best to check it out. The thing looked too small to be one of their heifers or young bulls, which had been calved in March. Now they were fully weaned and over four hundred pounds. No, the bundle ahead was something else. A small doe or a female wolf?

Once he and his ride had covered half the distance, Emmett realized this was no downed animal. The bundle in the road was a person, a woman.

Clicking his tongue to the roof of his mouth and gently tapping Bullet's sides with the heels of his boots, he urged the old boy to pick up the pace. Once he got next to the female, he leapt from his saddle and knelt down next to her.

Lying faceup, eyes closed, she was mumbling something. The first thing he saw was the gash just under her hairline. What was she doing this far from the paved road? He glanced around to see if he could see her car, but found none. What could've happened to her?

Her clothes were torn in a couple of spots and she had no shoes on her tiny feet. Even in her current state, he couldn't get over how unbelievably beautiful she was. Auburn hair framed her delicate facial features. Her thick red lips accentuated her pale skin. She was perfectly curvy, just the way he liked women.

"Are you awake, miss?"

Her mumbling continued but her eyes remained shut. He leaned down to see if he could make sense of her words.

"Right. Need to…bliss. Right…please help…bliss. Got to…right." She continued to ramble, but he couldn't make heads or tails out of what she was saying.

Her wound no longer bled, but had likely only just stopped. Dark blood coated her long auburn hair. He placed his fingers to her neck to see how steady her pulse was. Luckily, the beats vibrated evenly on his fingertips. Strong heart.

Moving her might be a risk since he wasn't sure if she had any internal injuries, but it was a risk he might have to take. The storm would be here in a flash and he couldn't, even if he stayed and covered her with his own frame, leave her in the middle of the road to be drenched. He moved his hands over her body, pressing slightly here and there to see if she had any broken bones or other wounds. Touching her slender arms and legs awakened strong emotions inside him—the need to protect, the need to possess, the need to claim.

He reined in his mind. This vision of feminine wonder needed him to remain focused. Once he was satisfied that he could move her and not harm her further, he swung the woman into his arms.

"Bullet, slow and easy. We don't want to hurt her."

His old friend turned his head and blinked. Emmett knew the

horse understood. Horses understood a lot more than most gave them credit for.

He hauled her up into the saddle with him, something he'd done several dozen times with other wounded creatures, but never with a woman before.

"You'll be okay, miss. I promise." A raindrop hit his nose. He placed his Stetson on her bloodied head to keep the coming rain out of her face. "Let's go, Bullet. Slow and easy."

* * * *

Cody Stone let out a big breath of relief as he drove his truck to the cabin. "Home sweet home."

"Amen to that, brother." Bryant, his twin, sat in the passenger's seat.

The rain was coming down so hard that the windshield wipers hadn't been able to keep up. He'd been driving blind for nearly an hour. His shoulders were tighter than he could ever remember them, and it wasn't from having to replace a half dozen posts and stringing new barbed wire for the fences either. It was from nerves about the possibility of rolling the truck on some pretty narrow roads. Dry, they were difficult. Wet, they were tough. Drenched, they were treacherous.

The lights were on in the cabin, indicating Emmett was already home. He looked up at the chimney and saw smoke coming out. Good deal. A fire was just what he needed for sure, and a few gulps of whiskey would warm up his insides real nice.

He stepped up on the cabin's front porch and heard the squeak of the board that needed a couple of nails in the worst way. His brothers and he had never wanted to repair it. Their mother had called it the cabin's doorbell years ago, and that had always brought a smile to their dads' faces. He liked the cabin better than their house down in the valley, where they stayed most of the time. The cabin was rustic and drafty in places. It didn't have Internet, or even a phone, but it held more memories for him than the house. He and his brothers had increased their stays up here over the years. Emmett claimed it was better to be on the ranch, especially during the winter and spring, than fifteen miles away. He was right, too. The roads often became impassable during snowstorms or downpours. The current rain would likely cause a slide of rock and mud—maybe two or three of them. Turkey's Pass would definitely need the Bobcat and probably Narrow Belt, too. Nickel Ridge might weather this storm without a mark, but the way the rain was coming down, he doubted it. That would mean at least six or seven days, at minimum, to clear the road to town. Not a problem. They had supplies enough to get through several months if need be.

With Bryant at his heels, Cody opened the door and entered the cabin. The fire was going, the lights were on, but there was no sign of Emmett.

"Bro, you surely haven't gone to bed already," he yelled down the short hallway that led to the two bedrooms on one side and their "playroom" on the other. The cabin's only bathroom was at the end of the hallway.

Emmett appeared from the bathroom and placed his index finger to his lips in the universal sign of "be quiet."

"Why? You got company back there?" He sure hoped so. It had been some time since he and his brothers had brought a female up here. Too long.

"Shhh. There's a woman back there," Emmett said in hushed tones. "She's injured. I found her on the road."

A million questions swirled in Cody's head. "Who is she?"

"I don't have a clue," he answered.

"Did you check for ID?" Bryant asked.

"None. She only had the clothes on her back, and they were in rough shape. Looks like she was in some sort of an accident, but I didn't see her car where I found her."

"Did you ask her who she was?" Cody knew the ranch was way off the beaten path and wondered how anyone would get so lost to end up on it.

"She's been out since I found her. Bad blow to the head. No broken bones that I can tell and no fever," his eldest brother answered. "I wiped off the grime as best I could. Then I put her in bed."

"Which bedroom?" he asked.

Emmett answered, "Mom and dads' room."

That figured. Even after all these years, none of them slept in there, keeping to the old routines from long ago before the accident. Unlike the house in the valley, where Emmett had claimed their parents' master suite, the cabin held an almost sacred quality for all of them. It was the spot that their family had enjoyed being together more than any other place on the planet.

Cody walked gingerly down the hall, keeping the squeaks from the floor to a minimum. He opened the door and peered into the space. The lamp on their dads' desk illuminated the room in a soft glow. Its warm light revealed a beautiful woman in bed. Her dark auburn hair covered the white pillow, which was stained with a little of her dried blood now. The wound on her forehead was at least three inches long, though it didn't detract one bit from her perfect features. He'd never uttered the word "stunning" before, but that was what she was. The heavy quilt, which had been given to their mother as a wedding gift by a distant relative, covered her. Her neck was slender, and her skin had a pearly hue, adding to the perfection his eyes were enjoying.

Though it might've been best to remove the woman's clothing to inspect her injuries more thoroughly, his brother hadn't. Typical Emmett. Always doing the *right* thing. He probably didn't want her to wake up completely stripped in a home full of strange men.

On the nightstand next to her was a bowl of water and the cloth his brother must have used to wash her.

Even clothed, her breasts pressed up against the covers, making it clear she was endowed in the manner he liked very much. Though he and his brothers enjoyed the whole feminine package and mystique, Bryant was definitely a leg man, Emmett a die-hard butt man, but Cody had always been drawn to the mouthwatering mounds of a woman's upper half, and this sweet lady's upper half was drool-worthy.

His cock tightened at the sight of this mystery woman. But along with the lust she'd ignited in him, there was something else, some other emotion, something powerful, something new. He tamped down his lust and went back to where he'd left his brothers.

"Holy hell, she's a knockout, Emmett."

"I know that look, Cody. I swear you're the most hopeless romantic of any man I've ever known." Emmett shook his head. "She's not some chick we found at the club in Destiny. She's not even from here. Best to keep that in mind."

"Maybe so, but I believe in long shots."

Bryant's eyebrows shot up. "A knockout, huh?"

"See for yourself," he told his twin.

As Bryant headed down the hallway, Emmett opened the liquor cabinet. "I just got her to bed. I need some fire in my belly. How about you?"

"For sure. Have you tried to wake her?"

"She was mumbling something when I found her, but she was never truly conscious. I haven't been able to get her to respond since. Whatever happened took a lot out of her. She needs to see a doctor."

Listening to the deluge outside, Cody knew getting her to Destiny and to Doc wasn't happening. "Nickel Ridge has got to be toast."

"Yep," Emmett said, clearly thinking the same thing as him. His brother got out three glasses, placed ice cubes in the first one, which was meant for him. Another he poured water in about a third of the way from the bottom. The last he left alone, save the Maker's Mark whiskey, which he also added to the other glasses. "Here you go,

Cody." Emmett handed him the straight-up glass.

"Fuck, she's got to be some kind of model," Bryant said, returning from his inspection of the woman. "I've never seen a more beautiful creature in my life."

"This is for you," Emmett said, handing his twin the glass with the added water.

"Thanks. God, I need it."

A loud boom of thunder shook the cabin, reminding them of the storm still outside.

"We all do," Emmett said.

Cody agreed, holding up his glass in front of him. "A toast, brothers."

"God, do you always have to be so dramatic?" Bryant asked.

"I do. Shut up and listen." Though he and his brothers had never voiced their feelings, there was a hole, a vacancy, an emptiness in their lives. He believed they felt it, too. They were brothers through thick and thin, good and bad—and, boy, there'd been a whole heap of bad—but as tight as their bond was, they'd lost so much after their parents' death. "To the woman in our cabin, may she recover fully under our care—"

"That's a great place to end a good toast," Emmett said.

"—and may she fall head over heels in love with us." Cody smiled and took a sip of his drink.

Bryant chuckled, but he knew his twin better than even Emmett did. Bryant, the quietest of the three of them, clearly liked the idea more than a little.

Emmett shook his head. "You should've stopped while you were ahead, Cody. We've got to make sure she's well. That's our first and only priority."

Something about his eldest brother's tone was different. Cody detected a hint of desire there. He sure hoped so. Hell, he even prayed so. With Emmett, the odds were slim, very slim.

# Chapter Two

Bryant Stone finished his whiskey and went to the kitchen to refill his glass. "What do we do now? There's no way we can get her to Doc in this weather."

His mind was racing, working out all the likely outcomes that bringing the wounded female to their cabin might result in. Cody had been right about her being beautiful. She was. Never had he seen such a specimen in his life. Curves to die for. Lips he would love to kiss for days and days. And more.

"The road's likely to be blocked after this storm." Cody downed the rest of his glass and walked up next to him. "We may not be able to get to town for at least a week."

"Don't sound so happy about it." Emmett sat down in Dad Trevor's chair. "She's hurt. Don't forget that. We're not doctors."

Bryant nodded, filling his glass. "He's right, you know. She might have a concussion. Do either of you know how to treat that?"

His brothers looked dumbstruck.

Emmett spoke first. "Should we use ice?"

"I remember something about the need to keep them awake," he said, keeping his worry pushed down.

"I couldn't wake her up earlier. Should we try again?" The panic in Emmett's voice was something new.

"Maybe we should get her in the tub and get her cleaned up." Cody's eyes seemed to hold both concern and lust at the idea. Bryant couldn't blame him. "We'll get a better idea about her injuries, and it might also get her to come to."

Emmett wasn't a man who was easily rattled. Back when his

eldest brother had fallen down the cliff and broken both his legs when they were all teenagers, it had been Emmett who remained levelheaded and saved the day by remaining calm. Definitely not Cody.

So seeing Emmett shook up about a stranger seemed way out of character for him.

"We should try to wake her first. If we can't, one of us needs to try to get down the road to the pay phone at the gas station. Doc won't be able to make it up here, but at least he can give us some advice on how to treat her." Emmett stood from his chair.

Bryant nodded. "Agreed."

Emmett and Cody thought he was the calmest of the three of them, even more than Emmett, but Bryant knew better. His outside might be granite, but his insides never ceased to churn.

"I just don't want to make things worse for her." Emmett sighed. "One of us should've taken the EMT training that old Sheriff Grayson asked us to take before he retired."

"The sheriff only wanted to get one of us under his thumb and you know it." Cody took the bottle from him and poured himself more whiskey. "Besides, we do know a thing or two about injuries and how to nurse someone back to health."

Emmett shook his head. "Not 'someone,' Cody. Some things. Animals. Livestock. She's a flesh-and-blood woman."

"And what nice flesh, too," Cody added.

Emmett stood and glared at Cody. "Get a fucking grip. This isn't some wish come true for us. We've got a woman who was in some kind of accident. We don't know who she is or where she comes from. Our responsibility, our only responsibility, is to try to do the best we can in a terrible situation. That's all. Nothing more. Do you understand me?"

Cody slammed his glass down. "Don't try to play dad to me, Emmett."

Bryant knew this song and dance well. Emmett and Cody

normally didn't clash, but when they did, when they saw a challenge from opposite sides, it could be World War Three. Like him, no doubt, their dicks were responding to the woman back in their parents' bedroom, creating a conflict with their minds—a virtual tug-of-war between instinct and rationale. Not what they needed now. Not one to normally step in between them, he knew he must. "Guys, aren't we getting ahead of ourselves?"

"Hello." A small, sweet voice from the hallway startled him.

He spun around and gazed at the most ravishing vision he'd ever seen. Wrapped in the quilt Emmett had placed on her, her bare feet stuck out from underneath the blanket. But it wasn't her little feet, tiny fingers, or pale skin that held his attention. As tantalizing as those were, it was her eyes that he couldn't stop staring into—wide with full lashes and the color of whiskey.

* * * *

Her head was pounding and her heart was racing. Was this some kind of nightmare? "Where am I?" she asked the three men. They all looked like they'd just stepped off of a Western movie set.

They rushed to her side, sending a wave of panic through her. She stepped back.

"You're in a cabin near Destiny, Colorado. Are you okay?" the one who looked to be the oldest asked.

She closed her eyes, trying to recall who he was to her. What came to her was emptiness. Her mind was blank. Zippo.

He was a dark-haired stranger with a cleft chin. Very handsome, yes, but alien. She had no recollection of him or the other two men.

"No." She wasn't okay. Nothing made sense. Even breathing was difficult, and she coughed several times.

"Let's get her back to bed," the tallest of the three said, placing his arm around her waist. Big brown eyes captured her with their intensity. He blinked his long lashes, mesmerizing her. Beautiful but rugged was the only way to describe such a man. His perfect lips were moving. Had he said something else?

"Wait. Please."

He tightened his hold on her. She wasn't sure what to do, but with her legs so wobbly, the added support had to be welcomed.

The need to clear her head, to know what was happening was even more agonizing than the pain in her body, which seemed to be coming from everywhere. "Who are you guys?"

"We're your rescuers, sweetheart," the mirror image of the man holding her said. Standing in front of her, he held out his hands for her to take.

"I'm either seeing double or you two are twins."

"Beautiful and smart to boot. You're quite the package, mystery lady. Yes, we're twins. I'm Cody Stone and the moody, quiet one holding you is Bryant. The guy on your right is Emmett, our big brother." Cody didn't wait for her to grab his hands but interlocked his thick, manly fingers in hers. "And who are you?"

What a simple question, one that any sane person should be able to answer without a single thought. She opened her mouth to tell him, but was shocked to realize she didn't have an answer. Slamming her lips together, she closed her eyes. It was on the tip of her tongue. *I am...*

Opening her eyes, suddenly her vision blurred and all the color of the room faded into a grayness. Her body chilled as a wave of iciness swept through her.

"Grab her," Cody said. "She's passing out."

* * * *

She coughed and felt the heaviness spin away. In its place came a brief calm, but as her consciousness took a better hold of her mind, the trance faded quickly, leaving only pain and fear.

"She's back with us." The voice, still unfamiliar to her, was from the cowboy who called himself Cody.

She forced her eyes open. "Yes. I'm awake. How long was I out?"

"Sixty seconds, tops." Another stranger. Why was she with people she didn't know?

She glanced over at the speaker, who was hovering on the right side of the bed, opposite Cody. His name was E-something. Emmett. That was it. Emmett's face was full of worry. Was it worry for her?

"I'd like to sit up." Being back in the bed she'd just left oddly comforted her. These three had clearly brought her back while she was out. It seemed as if they didn't mean her harm, but she couldn't be sure. In fact, she couldn't be sure of anything with a total memory that was less than thirty minutes long at the moment.

Cody's twin, Bryant, adjusted her pillow so that she could sit up slightly. "That better?" He brushed a lock of her hair out of her eyes.

"Much. Thank you."

"No need to talk, miss. Rest. We can figure all this out later." Cody smiled at her.

The pain in the top of her head made her wince. She reached up to touch the source, but Emmett's strong yet gentle hand stopped her from reaching it.

"Best not to do that." This guy was quite serious and self-assured. He clearly was familiar with taking charge. "It's just below your hairline, and I'm afraid it might start bleeding again."

"Okay." Her fingertips did find the lower strands of her hair. They were thick with dried blood. "Was I in an accident?"

Emmett nodded.

"What kind of accident?" She needed a bath to wash the mess out of her hair, but that would have to wait until she knew more. And her head quit pounding.

"I think an automobile accident, but I didn't see a car," Emmett answered. "I found you slumped over in the road by our property line just as this storm was coming on."

"Why here? Why not a hospital?" she asked, truly hoping to make sense of everything but having a difficult time.

"Rather than trying to get you to the clinic in Destiny, I decided to bring you to our cabin." Emmett seemed kind. "It's the best choice since the roads were already impassable."

She sighed. What kind of crazy dream was she living?

"Do you know why you were all the way up here? There's nothing much around these parts but ranches."

Closing her eyes, she tried to force her mind to pull up the memory. Nothing. Nada. "I don't remember anything before waking up in this bed. I don't even remember my name."

She could feel panic rising inside her. She took in a deep breath to calm herself and felt a pain in her chest, causing her to wince.

Bryant's hand touched her cheek. "That's probably from an airbag being deployed. That's our guess anyway. You don't appear to have any broken bones."

"Did I hit someone? Is anyone else hurt?"

Emmett shrugged. "You were the only one I found."

A bang of thunder shook the room and her. "How long has it been storming?"

"Over an hour, and it doesn't seem to be letting up."

"The storm has washed out all the roads, but we still need to get you into town to see the doc as soon as we can," Cody explained. "We must get you checked out."

"Can't you just call someone for help?" She didn't think she needed to see a doctor, but maybe the police could help her find her car. Then maybe she could find her ID and know who she was.

"There's no phone or Internet service this high up the mountain. We're stuck here for a while." Emmett seemed to be worried about the situation.

Cody walked to the door. "We'll have to make do until the rain stops. How about some tea, sweetheart?"

Her mouth felt like cotton. "Yes. I would love some."

"How do you like it?" he asked.

Another simple question but one she couldn't answer, her memory still lost to her. "I'm not sure."

"We'll all discover your likes and dislikes together." Emmett's tone was deep yet tender and comforting, too. "Make her three cups. One plain. One with sugar. One with cream."

"I'll make four. She might like cream and sugar."

"Good call."

Cody smiled and sent her a wink. "Everything is going to be just fine. You'll see."

She couldn't help but smile back at him. Stranger or not, the guy was charming, a kind of devil-may-care cowboy. Suddenly a bout of the shakes took hold of her. She couldn't stop trembling. Her skin felt cold.

Bryant leaned in and whispered, "Don't fret. This is normal. These shivers will end."

His words reached into her and the quakes subsided a little. "Are you a doctor?"

"No, but I won't let you down. I saw a lot of action in Afghanistan." Bryant took her hand. "We'll see you through this. You don't have a fever. That's good."

"You're a soldier?" Was he home on leave?

"Marine. I've been out for a couple of years." Bryant nodded toward the kitchen. "Cody and Emmett, too, though Emmett was in earlier than we were. He went to Iraq."

No wonder she felt so safe even though they were complete strangers. "Soldier cowboys came to my rescue. Someone should make a movie about that."

"Not a bad idea." Emmett glanced over at his brother. "I would've stayed in if I hadn't lost fifty percent of my hearing in my right ear from an IED exploding under my team."

Bryant squeezed her hand. "And Cody and I would've re-upped if you hadn't needed us to help at the ranch."

Emmett shrugged. "I would've managed with Sawyer and Reed

just fine. They're the best hands around. Besides, with the force reduction going on two years ago, I doubt either of you would've gotten an assignment."

"Why am I shaking?" She didn't expect an answer, only needed to voice the question.

"You've been through a helluva lot, miss." Bryant released her hand and pulled the covers up to her neck. "Nerves would be my bet. Who wouldn't be shaking after such a traumatic event?"

"But isn't that just it? I don't know what happened. You don't know what happened. I don't even know who I am or where I come from or where I was going." The trembles came back stronger and more frenzied than before. "What if I never gain my memory back?"

Emmett took a cloth from a bowl on the table by the bed. She hadn't even noticed it. He wrung it out and wiped her face. "You will. Bryant is right. Besides, someone as beautiful as you must have loved ones who will come looking for you. They'll help you sort things out. Until then, you're going to have to depend on us."

"My brother is right, miss. We may look rough around the edges, just three cowboys, but we won't let you down. Cross my heart." Bryant took his finger and traced an *X* over his manly chest. It was an action that seemed to reveal the boy he'd been long ago.

Her body wouldn't stop trembling as her mind continued to wrestle with itself. *Who am I?* The question rolled over again and again with no resolution. Her heart thudded in her chest hard and fast. "Emmett, you found me, right?"

"Yes."

"What else can you tell me that might jog my memory back into place?" She looked down at the tattered clothes she was wearing—slacks and a shirt. No shoes. "Was this all I had on?" They could've stripped her while she was out but hadn't. It made her feel better about them.

"You likely lost your shoes when you walked away in a daze from your car."

"What about a purse or identification?" She knew this was a feeble attempt to grasp at any shred that might pull her out of this nightmare, but she had to try.

Emmett shook his head. "Maybe this might help you remember. You were muttering something I didn't understand. What was it?" He rubbed his head and then snapped his fingers. "Right."

"Right what?" Bryant asked.

"That was one of the words she was saying over and over. Right and bliss. Does that help you?"

She sure wished it did, but it didn't spark a single thing in her locked-down brain. "No. Anything else, Emmett?"

He touched her cheek. "I'm sorry, but no."

Cody walked in carrying a tray with the four promised mugs. Each was steaming hot. "We don't have any fancy teas, sweetheart. I hope you like tried-and-true Lipton."

She held out her hand and saw the tremble of her fingers. Immediately, she recoiled her hand back. "Thank you, Cody. I'll drink it later."

"You'll drink it now, doll," he commanded. "You get to pick which cup, but once done, you'll drink all of it. Consider it your medicine." His I-mean-business tone was easy to detect, but his eyes sparkled with mischievousness that was not hard to miss.

"It will make you feel better," Bryant cajoled. "Might stop your trembles, too."

"Lucky me," she joked. "Three nurses disguised as cowboys. I'm not sure I'm really awake."

Bryant cupped her chin. "You're awake. And by the looks of you and the tone in your voice, I'd say you're doing well. Drink."

She had a feeling these cowboys could persuade her to do just about anything if they worked together. "Three against one isn't fair."

Emmett's fixed gaze unnerved her. "We never play fair, miss. Drink."

"Your bedside manners seem to be hardening." She laughed, her anxiety still present but a little less crushing. "I think I like the way you guys were earlier."

Cody sat on the bed, his weight depressing the mattress. He held one of the cups in front of her. "This one is straight. Nothing added."

"I surrender." All three cowboys' eyes seemed to light up. She took the cup from Cody and sipped the warm liquid. "It's fine."

"Not good enough. Try this one." He held out another cup. "This one is cream only."

Bryant took the first cup from her, and she curled her fingers around the new one, taking a quick sip. "Good. This will do."

"She's a tough one for sure." Emmett picked up one of the cups from the tray. "What's in this one?" he asked.

"Cream and sugar," Cody answered.

"Here," he said, handing it to her and taking away the cream-only cup. "I'm betting this will be the one you like the best."

"I like the other two just fine."

"Stubborn." Cody shook his head. "Perhaps that's what we should call you until you remember your name. What do you think, guys?"

She closed her eyes, searching her brain for any memories from before awakening here in this cabin. "I wish I could remember my name. You can't imagine how disconcerting that is to me."

"It's tough but you will remember. Trust us." Bryant's masculine face softened. "Now drink."

Even though they were strangers to her, she was feeling more comfortable with them. If they wanted to harm her, they could've easily done so even if she didn't have the bump on her head. They were men. Strong men. Muscled men. Powerful men. Three men. No way would she have any chance if their intentions were something dark and dangerous. Thankfully, they were being helpful and attentive, but they were also being intensely demanding and bullheaded. Still, they seemed kind and even sweet. She wanted to trust her instincts, but wasn't sure she should. Had her instincts worked for her in the past? Her muddled brain wouldn't release that or any other bit of information.

She took a sip of the cream-and-sugar cup of tea. The flavors exploded in her mouth in a familiar way. “This is it. I like cream and sugar in my tea. I think I’ve liked it for some time.” Excitement welled up in her.

“I knew it,” Emmett said, grinning from ear to ear. “What else do you remember?”

She closed her eyes and took another long drink, filling her mouth with the steamy goodness. Yes. She had enjoyed her tea with cream and sugar. But where? And when? Was that an odd combination in the United States? Had she visited England sometime? Why could she remember this was the United States but not her own name? Not her own home?

Another sip.

An image floated to her mind of a boy. A beautiful Hispanic boy. He was sitting in front of a television watching a cartoon, something about a dragon. He turned his head and smiled at her, warming her heart. What was his name? She fisted the cup with both hands, trying to call forth anything that might unlock her memories. Did this boy have anything to do with the accident? No. A single kernel of her past came to her. She’d been alone when this occurred. *What’s my name? What’s his name?*

“I’m remembering.” She sipped on the magic brew again. Still, she couldn’t call forth the boy’s name or hers, but they were linked somehow. She knew it down to her very core but wasn’t sure how or why. “I was alone when the accident happened.”

“Keep going, sweetheart.” Cody’s excitement shook his voice.

Another taste. Right and bliss? What did those words mean? Then the spell ended and the images vanished.

“That’s it. I saw a boy in front of a television set.”

“Your son, maybe?” Bryant asked.

“Perhaps.” Disappointment swept through her like a steamroller. She handed the empty cup back to Cody. “I’m not sure. Thank you for the tea."

"I've got an idea if you're up for it, sweetheart."

"No more tea. Please." Tea wasn't going to solve her problems.

"No." Cody shook his head. "How about a bath? It might unfasten those ties that are holding your memories from you."

The idea wasn't half bad. "Does your bathroom have a mirror?"

"Shit. We should've thought of that." Emmett opened a drawer and pulled out a hand mirror. "Seeing yourself might jog your memory."

"No," Bryant stated firmly. "She shouldn't see herself this way. Not with blood in her hair."

"I don't understand," she said.

"Put it away, Emmett," Bryant ordered. "Let's get her cleaned up, and then she can see her reflection and not until."

"You're going to clean me up?" Her nerves went into overdrive. "I can bathe myself, fellows." In fact, she wanted to. They were the only people she knew in the whole world at the moment, but they were still strangers to her. She was lost and alone until her mind healed, but she wasn't about to be stupid.

Cody touched her elbow. "Sweetheart—"

"My name is most definitely not 'sweetheart,' and I wish you'd stop calling me that." Her tone came out harsher than she'd meant it to.

His eyes saddened. "True. What shall we call you until we know your real name?"

Why was she being so rude to them? They'd only tried to help her. "I'm sorry, Cody. I'm just so upset about this. It's horrible not knowing who you are."

"It's okay. I understand." Apparently, he could be serious when necessary.

"Do you know your eyes are beautiful?" Emmett asked.

What did her eyes have to do with anything? "I haven't seen them, so no. I don't know. I'll trust that you're telling me the truth."

"I am." Emmett smiled. "They look like little pools of whiskey."

"Whiskey?" Where was he going with this?

"Would you mind if we called you 'Whiskey'?"

Bryant chuckled. "You've got absolutely no finesse when it comes to women, Emmett."

"Why do you say that? What's wrong with whiskey?" Emmett looked crushed.

"He's got a point, Bryant," Cody interjected. "All of us love whiskey. Kind of makes sense."

"You guys are too much." She smiled at the thought of getting named by these three cowboys. Even if it turned out to be only temporary, she might end up with a name that was better suited to a horse than a woman.

Bryant cupped her chin. "Amber. That's the color of your eyes. How would you like to be called 'Amber'?"

His eyes were mesmerizing. Cowboy hypnotist? Probably. "I like the name very much."

"Who knows?" Cody smiled. "Maybe that is your real name."

She laughed. "You're the worst of the three of you, aren't you?"

"Smart and beautiful," Cody said. "You like cream and sugar with your tea. What else are we going to learn about you, Amber?"

"Slow down, cowboy," Emmett said. "She's a newborn to this world. Let her get her bearings first."

Emmett was a smart man.

"Listen to your brother, Cody," she said. "I need to crawl before I can walk, okay?"

Cody twisted his mouth into a false frown and then smiled, warming her heart. "Okay, Amber. Now, about that bath?"

Bryant hit him on the back. "You're hopeless."

She laughed. "If you three promise to be gentlemen, I wouldn't mind a bath. I might need help though. I'm still pretty shaky."

"We'll be gentlemen, Amber," Emmett said and turned to his brothers. "Right?"

Bryant nodded.

"Always." Cody's eyes betrayed him.

He was definitely not used to being a gentleman, but she did think he could be trusted, if only for a single bath. She prayed she was right about him and his brothers. So far, they'd given her no reason not to trust them. Besides, what choice did she have at the moment? She had to depend on them for help until she recovered both in body and in mind.

"After my bath, I might want more of your delicious tea, Cody." Perhaps the bath and the tea might help her bring back the image of the boy. Surely if she could remember his name, she would be able to remember her own. "Would you mind brewing me more?"

"For you, Amber, I would travel to China to harvest the best teas in the world if it would evoke a single smile from your gorgeous lips."

Emmett snorted. "For the love of God, Cody, grow some balls."

"There's a lady present," Bryant snapped.

"Oh, you're right." Emmett cleared his throat. "Cody needs to grow a pair then. Better?"

Bryant shook his head. "Oh for God's sake."

"Emmett, women love poets, but you wouldn't know that." Cody turned to her. "Am I right, Amber?"

Memory or not, she was feeling better. "Depends if the poet is disguised as a cowboy or not."

# Chapter Three

Emmett carried Amber in his arms down the hallway to the bathroom. She'd tried to insist on walking herself, but after her fainting episode earlier, there was no way he would let her.

Bryant and Cody were inside the space, preparing it for her.

"Thank you for everything." She peered at him with her sweet eyes.

"My pleasure, sweetheart. Here we go."

He walked into the space that was filled with aromas of long ago. Apparently, his brothers had found some of their mother's bathing salts and scents. The big claw-foot tub had a little steam wafting up over its edge. The only light came from several candles placed strategically around the room.

"It's not too hot, is it?" he asked his brothers.

"Just moderately warm. Even though she doesn't have a temperature, best to be safe," Bryant said.

"Let me check the water, Amber. Ready to be put down for a second?" She was still a little pale and shaky. Emmett wished again that they'd been able to get her to a doctor.

Amber sighed. "I'm not an invalid, Emmett. Yes. I can stand on my own two feet."

She had spunk with a dose of contrariness. Just the perfect mix in a female he couldn't get enough of.

"Sassy lips can get you in trouble if you're not careful."

Her jaw dropped, and Emmett knew he'd pushed too hard and way too soon. A Dom knew when and when not to check limits in a woman, and this was definitely not the time to push. "Amber, keeping you safe is my only goal. When I found you on the road, I wasn't sure if you were dead or alive. Hell, even if we could get you to the hospital, they would be just as careful. Right?"

Amber lowered her eyes. "I'm sorry, Emmett. I'm not trying to be difficult. This is all so strange. I'll be sure to lean on you when you put me down. Will that work for you?"

Again, his cock and balls applauded her submissive nature that was showing itself so deliciously with every tremble, every word, every sigh. "That will please me very much."

He lowered her to the floor, and she did as promised, leaning into him. He bent down and sent his hand into the water. It was just the right temperature.

"Nice job, guys," he said.

Cody snorted. "Glad it meets with your approval. Now, let's hear how the only one that matters feels about the bath. Amber, what do you think?"

Keeping one arm around her breasts, Amber placed the hand of the other arm in the water next to Emmett's hand. How he wanted to interlock his fingers with hers, but of course he didn't. Removing his hand from the bath, he watched as her slender fingers disturbed the water and imagined what it would feel like to have her clawing his back with them.

Amber turned and gave his brother a little smile. "It's perfect, Cody. Thank you. You guys are so sweet to do this for me. A stranger. I'm so grateful."

Emmett wanted to press his lips to hers, to taste her mouth, to send his tongue into her. But he didn't. His cock hated him for it, but it was the right thing to do. Amber might be attached. She might even be married. The boy she mentioned remembering might be her son from some lucky man.

The possessive streak that had grown inside him since finding her was now a lumbering, angry giant. He couldn't imagine ever allowing any man, husband or not, to touch her. But that wasn't sane or even part of his makeup. He and his brothers had found a home, a way of being, a lifestyle that made sense of the world, at Phase Four, Destiny's local BDSM club. If another had a claim on Amber, he must honor it even if it meant his whole being would be ripped into shreds. It was the right thing to do. But if she was free, she wouldn't be for long. He'd see to that. Until they knew, there would be no touches, no kisses, and definitely no fucking.

"Your clothes will have to go, Amber."

Her cheeks turned red, and she blinked several times.

He wasn't taking any chances. "I'll stay with you to make sure you don't fall."

Amber's face flushed. "I'm good enough to get in the tub myself, Emmett."

"Even a little dizzy is too much. I'm staying. I won't look at your body while you undress. Just your eyes." He wanted her to trust him. Despite his cock's sudden throbbing, he was a man of his word. "Once in the tub, I will turn around to give you some privacy, but I will remain in the room. Until we're certain your condition is stable, that's how things will have to be."

"That's not much privacy, cowboy, if you ask me," she said meekly.

God, he could listen to her sweet voice day in and day out and never tire of it. "You're safe with me. Understand?"

Her stare tangled with his, causing more heat to move down into his jeans.

"I believe you," Amber whispered.

"We don't want you to sue us if you trip and bust your head, sweetheart," Cody joked.

She smirked. "Fine."

* * * *

Amber knew she wouldn't get anywhere arguing to be left alone.

Emmett was staying. Emmett, her savior. Emmett, the cowboy. Emmett, the stranger.

Was she being silly about being so modest? He could've stripped her of her clothes while she'd been out but hadn't. She couldn't know for sure, but he seemed a perfect gentleman.

She turned to Bryant and Cody. "What about you two?"

"Until you're safe and sound in the bath, I'm staying," Cody informed her.

"Same here, Amber. But once you're in, we'll leave." Bryant seemed as if he could read her mind.

Amber seemed to accept her fate. "Will you guys close your eyes while Emmett helps me in? I know it sounds silly, but would you, please?"

"Of course." Bryant's eyes shut.

Cody stood there, apparently struggling with her request. Then he did close his eyes.

"Thank you," she said softly.

"Are we supposed to keep them closed until you're in the water?" Cody asked.

"That would be nice."

Cody shrugged. She wouldn't be surprised if he opened his eyelids ever so slightly to take a peek. Bryant's were shut tight. They might look the same but they most certainly were different in other ways.

She looked into Emmett's mesmerizing orbs. "I'm ready."

He nodded. "Clothes off, Amber."

She obeyed, removing her shirt first, then slipping out of her slacks. She tossed them to the floor. Emmett's eyes never left hers, thankfully. He was a man who kept his word, but she suspected there was something quite dangerous he could release should he choose.

"The rest," he said firmly. "And inspect your body for any other injuries. I don't expect any, but I want you to look closely just in case."

Why did it seem so natural, so right to do as he asked? She wasn't sure but it most certainly did. Her fingers trembled as she unfastened her bra. She glanced down at her body as he'd ordered. Not a scratch. Raising her eyes back to his, she was relieved to see his hadn't moved south, not even a fraction of an inch. Still, she knew he could see peripherally some of her body. She hesitated for a moment before slipping off her panties. A massive quiver rolled through her.

"Ready for your bath?" he asked tenderly.

She nodded, shivering from head to toe.

He lifted her into his arms and stepped up to the beautiful antique bath. His rough fingers on her naked skin were an incredible assault on her senses, even more than the inviting water. Tears brimmed her eyes at the tenderness of these rugged cowboys. They were treating her like a princess, even though none of them—and that included Amber—knew who she was.

Her bottom was the first to experience the warmth of the bath. The temperature was perfect—not too hot or too cold. It backed down her shivers. Emmett lowered her fully into the luscious liquid. The water felt amazing on her skin, but her trembles, though muted, continued.

"Is it warm enough for you, Amber?" Bryant asked, eyes still closed.

"Wonderful." Then something more sensible slammed her with a new set of shivers. What if they were responsible for her current state? What if they'd drugged her or worse? What did she really know about them? Not a damn thing. In her heart, she believed them to be trustworthy, but was she being smart? What kind of person followed their heart? Had that been the reason she'd ended up in this awful situation in the first place? "Okay, I'm in. May I have that privacy you promised now?"

Cody's eyes opened, and he fixed his hot gaze on her. The corners of his mouth turned up slightly, showing her his approval of what he saw and pleasing her more than a little.

"Please, Cody. You promised." She covered her breasts with both hands.

His eyes slammed shut. "You sure, sweetheart?"

"I need time to think. Perhaps my memory will come back."

"Of course you need time, Amber." Bryant's eyes remained closed.

"We'll be just outside the door," Cody said. "In case Emmett needs help with you."

She studied his face, checking for any sign he might be stealing another glance, but found none. She grinned. "You're a devil, Cody."

"I can handle things here." Emmett's tone had a strand of anger threaded through it. Of the three, he seemed the most quick to explode.

"Don't let her get out of the bath by herself." Obviously, Cody enjoyed goading his eldest brother very much.

"Chill out. Both of you." Bryant, eyes still closed, tilted his head in her direction. "We'll leave, Amber. We'll be just outside the door should you need us."

Bryant was the quietest of the three, staying back until a referee was needed, which it seemed might be more often than not.

She looked up at Emmett. His eyes remained open and locked in on hers. "You said you would turn away, cowboy."

"Yes, I did." He sat on the commode, facing the wall. "Time for you guys to leave."

"Are you hungry, Amber?" Bryant asked.

Her stomach rumbled in response. "Yes. A little."

Bryant laughed, obviously hearing the sound. "More than a little, I bet. How does a thick, juicy steak sound?"

"She might be a vegetarian," Cody mocked. "That would be a bad idea. How about some pasta instead?"

The banter was part of the charm of these three. They clearly cared for each other. That was quite evident.

"Even if I was before, Cody, I can be anything now. Steak sounds just fine, Bryant. Pasta would be great, too. I'm actually starving."

"Time for a feast then. I'm really hungry, myself," Emmett said.

"What do you take us for, bro? Short-order cooks?" Cody shook his head, and still his eyes were battened down.

"Your cooking talents leave a lot to be desired, but beggars must take what they're offered." Emmett laughed. "Amber deserves a delicious meal, not more of your slop."

"I've had it with your crap." Cody was smiling, as was Bryant. Even without her memories, she could tell this teasing was something the Stones enjoyed often. It seemed to be their way of expressing affection, which was clearly overflowing. "You're no better than I am in the kitchen."

"How about you, Bryant? You know anything about food prep?" she asked as her belly growled even louder than before.

Bryant shook his head. "None of us really do. We're more microwave guys than anything. I'm not too bad with the grill outside, but that's definitely off the table because of the storm. Burgers, hot dogs, and steak usually turn out fine. Anything else…not so much."

"What my twin is not telling you, sweetheart, is if you don't mind chewing until your jaw aches, you will love his shoe leather…I mean food." Cody laughed.

"What are you now? Destiny Daily's local food critique?" Bryant asked. "You've never complained before."

She had to stop this. "Fellows, it will be fine. I'm hungry. Anything will do. I'm sure whatever you prepare will be delicious."

"I promise to do my best." Bryant's tone lacked the confidence she'd heard from him before about other things. She wasn't sure what kind of meal he would be serving, but she didn't mind. Had she ever been so famished before? No recollection.

"Me, too, sweetheart," Cody said.

"We've interrupted Amber's private time." Bryant smiled, and her heart melted. "Let's get her dinner ready and give her privacy." He tilted his head to her. "Do you need anything?"

She shook her head. "Thank you."

"I'm going to leave the door open in case we're needed," Cody said. "That way we can hear you if you call."

"I've got this," Emmett growled.

"I'm still leaving the door open," Cody said. He didn't seem concerned with Emmett's sullen tone.

With his charm and confidence, Cody would be easy to fall for. "Overprotective much?" She couldn't help but grin.

Cody shrugged. "With you, apparently I am."

Bryant and Cody exited the room, keeping their words about not looking. She sighed.

"You okay, Amber?" Emmett said, his back still to her.

They were all overprotective, it seemed. "I'm fine, cowboy. I'm fine."

"Take your time. I won't rush you. But if you need anything, just say the word. Understand?"

"Yes. I understand." Her body seemed to respond to his forceful words in ways that both surprised and thrilled her. Her skin tingled and not from the warmth of the water.

"Check in with me every so often so I know you're okay. I don't want you passing out in the tub."

"I will. You've got to trust me, too, Emmett. I'm no fool." Although without her memories, she couldn't be sure that was true.

"Okay then," he said. "Enjoy your bath, Amber."

"I will, cowboy. I will."

He and his brothers were her whole world for the time being, at the very least until her memory returned. What choice did she have but to trust them? But more than that, she did trust them. Call it instinct, intuition, impulse, or whatever. She truly trusted them. They might be capable of some terrible things, but she couldn't envision them doing anything that would harm her.

She grabbed the sponge on the side of the tub and plunged it beneath the water's surface. Her thoughts were buzzing, though landing on no memory. Where did she come from? Why was she here? What accident had caused this? She closed her eyes, took a deep breath, and moved down into the tub until her head was completely submerged. The image of the young boy floated through her mind's eye. Something about this boy had to be important, but what? Who was he? Where was he? Then the apparition vanished. Trying to will the youth's reflection back, she remained down in the water. But her injured head had no sway over what memories were locked away. *Please. I want to remember.* Nothing. When her lungs demanded oxygen, she pushed her upper body out of the water.

"What kind of person am I?" she asked herself silently, knowing Emmett was right there, ready to jump at her least little request.

She squeezed shampoo from the container into her hand. As she washed her hair, Amber considered several questions rolling through her mind, but one in particular stayed in the forefront, demanding an answer that just wouldn't come. *Who am I?*

She didn't have a clue. Not even one. Sinner or saint? Who knew? Maybe her past life was too awful, too painful to return to. Had she been running from something—or someone? Could having one's memory wiped clean be a blessing, a restart, or some kind of new birth? Maybe. Still, she wanted to know something. A thread. A crumb. What about the boy? Was that a true memory or some fantasy her addled brain had produced? Again, the broken synaptic paths in her brain remained painfully mute on the subject.

Plunging back under the water, she threaded her hands through her long hair, rinsing each strand of the shampoo. The only memories that came from this submerging were of the past hour, memories of the three cowboys who were so attentive, so kind, and so damn good looking—incredibly so.

She came up for a much-needed breath. She squeezed out the water in her hair. "What can I do to fix this?" she asked aloud.

Instantly, Emmett was by her side. "What do you need, Amber?" His face stormed with obvious worry.

Smiling, she shook her head. "Apparently, I'm the kind of person who talks to themselves when trying to solve a problem. I might be crazy, you know. Would you happen to have a straightjacket handy?"

"You're definitely not crazy," he said with a tone of authority that hit her between the eyes. Even his stare was emphatic when it came to his belief in her mental capacity.

She wasn't so sure. Perhaps she had escaped some kind of mental institution. Anything was possible. Absolutely anything. "And how would you know?"

"Believe me, I know crazy, which isn't what you are. You sure you don't need anything?" His eyes, his beautiful eyes, were two tiny windows she couldn't bear to look away from.

"I'm really good. Feeling better, too. Who knows? Maybe this bath will bring back my past."

He touched her cheek so gently. "If that's what's best for you, then I hope it happens, sweetheart. I'll be one step away." He went back to his guard post on the porcelain.

# Chapter Four

Amber's mind drifted. Emmett was so quiet she couldn't even hear his breathing. She closed her eyes, and a towering wall stood in front of her. On the other side of that imaginary wall was her past, her thoughts, her memories, and who knew what else.

Time alone.

Time to figure out what she did know and if she was crazy or not. How could she get past this wall? There seemed to be no door anywhere. It was too tall to climb. In her gut, she knew it was too deep to dig under, too thick to crush. The more she thought about the thing, the more dread, awful and sobering, welled up inside her. Emmett had said words that reached into her very bones and made her wonder if she should leave well enough alone. "If that's what's best for you…"

Had she built the wall as a defense to some terrible past?

*What do I know?*

She was a woman. She was American. Holding up her hands in front of her eyes, she counted ten fingers. Raising her feet out of the warm water, she wiggled her ten toes. *Good.* Auburn hair. Other than those few facts, she didn't know a damn thing about her past, and that was terrifying and frustrating. Was someone looking for her? The rainstorm continued outside, mocking her with every crash of thunder.

This was the twenty-first century, for crying out loud. Women didn't act like helpless damsels who needed big, tough cowboys to save them. Why was she surrendering so quickly to their rescue? Then it hit her. *It's the twenty-first century. I remembered that.* If she could recall that fact, couldn't she recall more? It made sense—quite a lot of sense.

Excitement rolled through her as hope flamed hot. *I'm going to remember.* She would allow herself the pleasure of a short soak. The culinary-challenged cowboys were certainly still working on her meal. She would eat every bite. They deserved that from her at the very least for all they'd done for her.

She bent her knees slightly, slipping down into the water until all that remained above the shiny surface was her head. The tension she'd felt in her muscles began to fade. Even the ache in her forehead softened. She drifted into a hazy, warm state of consciousness. The wall was gone, thankfully. It was too scary to deal with now. Why not enjoy this amazing bath and let her worries fade? Every speck of strain in her body released and softened. Her shoulders slumped, her breathing relaxed, and her eyes grew so very heavy. Lingering in the warm water, she succumbed to her fatigue. Gone was the worry of who she was or where she'd come from. In its place came softening thoughts. Drifting into a delicious, trancelike state, the world faded into the background. Gone was the claw-foot tub and warm water. Gone, too, was her pain. Memories didn't matter in this space of steam and dreams. The sensation of floating weightlessly seemed so very real.

Emmett's face appeared, strong and confident. A little sigh left her lips. He was holding her in the road again, only this time, he was naked and so was she. His thick, manly lips came crashing down on hers with a force that caused her entire body to shudder, but the bulk of the quivering remained deep inside her pussy.

"Amber, you are so beautiful." His words were masculine and truthful.

"You've saved me." Her words came out lyrical and full of breathy passion.

She stared up at him, and her body temperature rose several degrees. He lowered her down onto a soft white blanket in the middle of a meadow. The sun was low in the horizon, highlighting his bronzed skin perfectly. The air remained nice and steamy. His hands came down on her breasts, causing her to gasp delightfully. His thick fingers massaged her mounds with a skill that defied logic and reason. Each tiny swirl of his fingertips shot through her like bullets of desire, raising her need, her want, her craving to levels that shouldn't be possible, and yet he pushed her even more. How did he know exactly what to do to get her body to respond so? He'd saved her, and she wanted to give him his reward—all of it. In return, she, too, would be rewarded.

He nuzzled into her neck, causing her skin to stand up and tingle with hot electricity. His hands moved down her body with an ease and deliberateness that told her he meant to take his time, a lot of time. Emmett's lovemaking meant something and she knew she would never be the same once he was inside her, claiming her for always.

With her eyes closed, she moved the sponge over her skin. Where it touched—where Emmett touched—tingles came, grew, and intensified.

"Hey, baby." Cody touched her cheek.

"Hi," she answered. Being between him and Emmett on the blanket felt so right, so wonderful, so necessary. Her body began to respond, heating up wherever the men touched her. Every care vanished inside her. Her pussy began to ache and her clit began to throb. She couldn't keep still, need clawing at the very fabric of her being.

Feeling Bryant underneath her multiplied the fantasy until she thought she could stand no more. He tugged on her hair, forcing her to tilt her head up until they locked eyes. "Amber, we're here for you. Always. You're ours."

Emmett and Cody nodded their agreement.

When would they take her, really take her? She was theirs. They'd saved her. More than that, they'd been there for her in every way. Kind. Loving. Manly. Honest. Had she ever known any men like them before?

Six hands massaged her body into a total frenzy of sensations. “Please. Please. I need you.” The truthful resonation of her own breathy words was filled with impact, resolve, and submission. A thirst, so powerful and all-consuming, swept through her like a tsunami. Fiery electricity rolled through her as they kissed, licked, caressed every inch of her skin. No part of her body was safe from them, and she happily waved the white flag of surrender to her cowboy conquerors.

“Amber, I want to be inside you.” Emmett growled beside her.

“I want that, too,” she confessed freely.

He kissed her again, filling her mouth with his hot, lusty tongue. He tasted of long rides and warm nights. His weight felt so good on top of her. The aching in her pussy grew and grew to the unbearable. Her clit’s pulsing drove her to the brink of madness. “Please, Emmett. Please. Do it.”

Moving her fingers to her pussy, she felt his thick, long cock pierce her sex, filling her utterly, completely, and absolutely. “Yes. Yes. Yes.” More like breaths than words, she continued panting as he moved deeper and deeper into her body. Her savior, her cowboy, her man. Emmett Stone. Emmett. And then her climax shook every cell in her body, from head to toe and back again. Remaining still and quiet was impossible. Her responses came and came and came, filling her with a myriad of sensations. “Yes. Yes. Yes.” The words ran through her mind over and over.

Emmett had found her and brought her to his brothers. Without these men, she would’ve died, most certainly. She owed them her very life at the least. “Emmett. Thank you,” she said as her orgasm softened to a nice warm hum.

“For what?” he asked.

Her eyes popped open, and she could feel her heart thudding hard in her chest. The dream receded into the back of her mind. The water was still warm, but the steam was gone. She turned and saw Emmett, no longer sitting with his back to her but now facing her directly. She glanced back at the water, feeling her cheeks heat up. When she saw where her hand was at that very moment, they flamed to bonfire temperatures. Her hand was between her legs. She jerked it back to her chest, causing the still water to be disturbed.

"You okay, Amber?" he asked.

"Fine. Could you hand me a towel and then go back to facing the wall again?"

"Towel? Yes. Wall? I'm done with that. Besides, I think you're ready to get out, and like I said earlier, you will be accepting my help for that. Understand?"

Denying Emmett anything he wanted would be next to impossible for her, though she wasn't about to tell him that. "I'm sure I'm fine."

* * * *

Emmett stared at Amber. His cock and balls ached and throbbed in his jeans. After witnessing her slip off into what was clearly an erotic dream of some sort, his lust had gone into overdrive, pressing the pedal to the floor. "Fine or not, you will not get out of that tub without me."

"You like giving orders, don't you, cowboy?"

He stood and walked to the side of the tub, making sure to keep his eyes directly on hers. "Think what you like, honey. I will not have you fall on my watch. Got it?" God, keeping his head around her was proving to be more difficult than he could imagine.

She smiled and sent him a mock salute. "About that towel?"

"First, let's get you on your feet." He bent down and lifted her out of the tub. Amber felt so good in his arms. "Don't let go of me, sweetheart." He lowered her down until she was standing, though still with her fingers wrapped around his neck. Her obedience fueled even more hunger inside him. He grabbed one of the towels on the shelf by them and wrapped it around her body.

"Thank you, Emmett."

Hearing her say his name was heaven. “You’re more than welcome, Amber. Okay, you can let go now.” She did, and he grabbed another towel. “Time to dry your lovely locks.”

“Who calls hair ‘locks’?”

“I do. My brothers do. This is rural Colorado. This isn’t Denver.”

“I’m not an invalid. I can do some things myself like drying my own hair.” She winked, and his balls grew even heavier.

“Perhaps, but that doesn’t change that I’m drying you off.” He had no idea why he was coming on so strong. Why not let her towel off by herself? She seemed strong enough to stand on her own. If not, he could stay and catch her. Why not? Because he knew what he had to do. He knew what was best. Always had. Besides, drying her off would be his pleasure, even though it must remain on the up-and-up.

Being right and confident all the time had been his curse ever since losing his parents in the plane crash. The questioning and uncertain boy he’d been prior to their deaths had melted into nothingness, replaced by the person needed to keep him and his brothers together. Necessity had created the man he’d become, but time had grown the roots deep into his soul. Doubt didn’t hold a place inside him—couldn’t. Until Amber.

He toweled her long, lush hair, inhaling its coconut fragrance. Then he moved on to drying her soft, pale skin, imagining what it would feel like to touch such delicate flesh.

Women had a place in his world, and that place was at Phase Four. One day in the future, he and his brothers would choose one for a more permanent arrangement. At least that was what he’d imagined would happen—until her. Such a plan seemed jaded and naïve now.

“You’re sure doing a thorough job, cowboy.”

“I don’t want you catching a cold, Amber.”

Had his fathers selected his mother like some kind of prize heifer at the livestock auction? Of course not. He knew their story well. Before the accident, they’d told it often to him and his twin brothers. What a whirlwind of excitement and passion. Their mother was from

Texas, not Destiny. She'd come to teach at the one-room schoolhouse. "It was love at first sight, boys," Dad Rich had always said, causing Mom to blush and giggle.

"You're miles away, aren't you, cowboy?" Amber's eyes sparkled.

"I guess I am." He continued stroking her arms with the towel, though they were sufficiently dry. Maybe he was simply unwilling to end this intimate time with her, even though nothing wicked would come of it—couldn't come of it. He'd lost his faith in possibilities, in dreams, in magic long ago. Facts made sense to him. Plans were his guide. Struggle was its own reward. Love at first sight? For his parents, yes. Not for him.

"There you go again, Emmett." She smiled, and he knew that she had the power to bring sunshine. "What's got your mind tied up in knots?"

Great description, though he would much rather see her tied up in his knots. "I'm wondering how long this rainstorm is going to go on for." The playroom needed to be locked up. No sense in scaring Amber more than she'd already been. He made a mental note to do just that while she was eating her meal. "Almost finished." He knelt down in front of her. She kept a towel around her as he dried off her silky legs with another. "What's going through your mind? You seem better than earlier."

She frowned, which made his gut tighten. The last thing he wanted to do was cause her pain. His question had been an idiotic one. Her mind was not her own. Her memories were gone, and he'd been stupid to remind her of that fact by his inquiry.

"You're furrowing your brow, cowboy. Your question didn't bother me, just made me pause for a moment."

"Sorry, Amber. Too long in the saddle today, I guess. It's been a long time since this old cabin had a real woman in it." Loneliness was a constant companion of his. It wasn't something he voiced aloud to anyone, even his brothers, but it was true. Having her here lifted a gray cloud inside him.

"I seriously doubt that. I did realize that I haven't lost my entire mind. This is the United States, right?"

"Sure thing. Destiny is in Northwestern Colorado, almost to the Wyoming border. We're deep in the heart of the Rocky Mountains." The rain continued outside, reminding him it would be several days, if not a week or more, before he could take her to town. "Let's get you some clean clothes." He guided her to sit on the seat of the commode. "I'll be right back."

All his mother's clothes were still at the house in town. He found a shirt and a pair of jeans from when the twins were teenagers, still too big for Amber, but they would have to suffice. He rushed back to the bathroom and found her just where he'd left her. She smiled at him, and his heart was hers.

"You think that will fit me?" she asked.

"It will keep you warm, sweetheart."

"Thank you, Emmett." Her voice cracked with apparent sudden emotion. "I'm not sure if I can ever repay you for what you and your brothers have done for me."

Had he ever met a woman so upbeat and full of life? She was gutsy and brave and definitely not a pushover. She'd lost her memory, but instead of breaking down and crying, she was working hard to regain it. She'd been brave and trusted him and his brothers even when she should have been scared of them. Taming someone like her would be any Dom's pleasure, but she wasn't one of the subs at Phase Four. She could be someone's wife or girlfriend or fiancée. Until he knew, it had to be hands off. That was how it was, whether he liked it or not.

"Sweetheart, there's nothing you need to do. We're happy to help." More than happy. Could he let himself dream? He shouldn't but couldn't resist as he helped her on with the shirt.

The conversation with his two dads the week before their unfortunate death came back to him with a clarity that made it feel as if it had occurred a moment ago and not twelve years earlier. They'd spent time with him and his brothers discussing what it really meant for men to share a woman. God, how he would love to share Amber with his brothers. She was so perfect for all of them. Bright. Sweet. Kind. If only he knew if she were unattached or not, then he could know whether to let down his guard and put on the full-court press.

She stepped back and looked at herself in the mirror, tilting her head from side to side, obviously trying to decide what she looked like in the clothes.

Seeing her dressed in a teenage boy's shirt added to her allure. She gripped the jeans, which were far too long for her to wear anywhere but indoors. "What do you think, Emmett?"

"You look amazing."

"You're just saying that, but I'll take it."

He looked at her bare feet, delicate and sweet, on the tiled floor. Instead of thinking about getting her some socks, his possessive lust shot up, causing his gut to tighten and his cock to throb.

"Are you hungry, Emmett?" she asked innocently. God, if she only knew what she was asking.

"I am. Are you?"

She turned and nodded.

Silently, he'd craved what his parents had and had listened intently to the fatherly advice all those years ago. Cody and Bryant had been riveted by the discussion, though of course Cody, ever the romantic, had tons of questions for their dads.

His brothers were completely lost to her, acting like cavemen or more like two lovesick schoolboys. Hell, those two were in the kitchen cooking. Cooking? Neither of them had a clue about what went on in a kitchen beyond grabbing a beer from the fridge or nuking something in the microwave for a quick hot meal. What in the world they were going to present to Amber to eat, he had no idea.

When it came to Amber, Cody was going to be hard to rein in, Bryant, a bit easier, though Emmett had seen something in his eyes that might mean trouble. He didn't want to disappoint his brothers. God knew how much they'd suffered. But he had to be the responsible one. They depended on him. Better to do the right thing and keep the pain to a minimum than to give in to long-buried hopes and be tortured by the loss. Until they knew more, hands off.

"There you go again, Emmett. Off on some thought vacation." She giggled, and his hard heart melted inside his chest.

Marriage had seemed so distant, in the faraway future. There were plenty of wild oats to sow still. Until Amber.

"Let's go see what my two brothers have burnt for you." He grabbed her hand and led her out of the bathroom. Silently, he hoped against all odds that Amber didn't have a claim on her by any other man.

# Chapter Five

Amber inhaled the delicious aromas of the food Cody and Bryant had prepared for her before actually seeing the meal. "Wow, this is quite the meal, fellows."

Cody smiled and pulled out a chair from the kitchen table. "Sweetheart, this is for you."

"Thank you." The table was filled with trays of eggs, prepared in every fashion possible—scrambled, fried, sunny-side-up, poached, and even boiled. On another tray was a pile of crisp bacon that couldn't dare hold another piece. Fresh biscuits were in a breadbasket next to a bowl of cream gravy. Three kinds of jam sat next to her bone-white plate, the only one on the table. A pitcher of orange juice was paired with a carafe that she guessed was filled with hot coffee. "This is way too much. Are you going to make me eat this all by myself?"

Emmett shook his head. "Dumb-asses, you forgot to set plates for us. I thought you were starving."

Cody punched his eldest brother in the arm. "Ladies first, or have you forgot your manners?"

She sat in the chair Cody was holding for her. "Seriously, I would like you guys to join me. It would be strange to eat while you watch."

"I, for one, am starving. I can't believe you two pulled this off," Emmett said, opening the cabinet closest to him and pulling out three plates.

"I know it's dinnertime, but breakfast foods are my specialty," Cody said, taking the seat next to her.

Bryant smiled and sat in the seat opposite her, leaving the other side for Emmett.

Amber stared at the feast. “Thank you so much.”

“Enjoy,” Bryant said, motioning her to dive in.

She did, loading her plate to the brim. Emmett filled her juice glass up with the OJ, and Cody poured her a cup of steamy coffee.

They didn’t move to fill their plates, but instead were staring at her like a jury of three.

“Cowboys,” she mocked. “I never knew they were so demanding. I suppose you won’t fill your plates until I’ve at least taken a bite. Is that it?”

“Smart girl.” Cody grabbed her hand and squeezed. “And you can’t imagine how demanding we can be, sweetheart.”

“That’s enough,” Emmett growled. “Let her eat her meal in peace, Cody.”

What was it about these two that kept them on edge? Was it something about her? She wasn’t sure, but the tension was thick between them.

Hoping to relax the strain, she took a bite of the biscuit she’d placed on her plate. It was flaky and warm. “Yummy.”

Bryant grinned and Cody nodded. They had clearly been worried about what they’d put in front of her to eat. She found that so very sweet of them.

Then like a pack of wolves, they filled their plates and began devouring food at a breakneck pace. She’d finished about half her plate and they were all refilling their plates.

“Not bad, guys,” Emmett said. “You two have been holding out on me. Who taught you to cook like this? Wait. I remember.” His face darkened with an apparent heavy weight.

Cody frowned. “Mom.”

“Right.”

Bryant pushed his empty plate forward. “Saturday mornings.”

“She would’ve been proud of this spread, guys.” Emmett grabbed the carafe. “More coffee, Amber?”

She didn't know what had happened to their mom, but it was obvious to Amber they all missed her very much. "No, thank you. I'm so full. It was amazing. Thank you, guys. I can at least manage the cleanup."

"Not a chance," Cody said, standing. "We're going to wait on you, princess."

"I agree." Emmett brushed the hair out of her eyes, causing a little tingle to shoot up her spine. "You've been through quite an ordeal, Amber. Give it a few days before you try to get back to normal."

"What's normal for me, cowboy? I sure don't know what that is." In her mind, the wall she'd imagined earlier appeared again. It mocked her, keeping her from her memories, which were just on the other side. How to get over the wall?

"Sweetheart, you have to be patient." Bryant's tone was firm but comforting. "We all have to be. I'm sure whatever is locked away in your pretty little head won't be for long. Trust me."

"I wish something would trigger a memory." She thought about how their demeanors had changed when they'd been talking about their mother. What about her family? Maybe if she asked them questions, it would help her recall something. "Do you have a picture of your parents? I'd like to see what this woman who taught you guys how to make such an amazing breakfast looked like."

"That's a great idea." Cody grabbed up the empty plates and placed them into the sink. "Bryant, go get their wedding picture. It's on the bookshelf in our bedroom."

"Got it." He jumped up and headed down the hallway.

"What was your mom's name?" she asked Emmett, who was still sitting next to her.

"Beverly," he said with a tinge of awe. "She was from Texas."

"Did your dad meet her there?"

Before he could answer, Bryant was back with the framed photo. He handed it to her.

She stared at the picture. An auburn-haired bride stood between two men in tuxedos. “Which one is your dad?”

“They both are,” Emmett said flatly. “This is Dad Rich.” He pointed to the man to the left of his mother. “And this guy is Dad Trevor.”

“I’m confused. You have two dads?”

“Had. Yes, sweetheart. Have you ever heard of plural marriages before?”

Her muddled mind was able to call up a single word that told her she did. “Bigamy.”

Cody continued to clear dishes from the table. “That word usually implies something different than what we grew up with. There were no secrets between our dads and our mom.”

“Amber, things are quite different around here than in the outside world.” Bryant’s eyes were fixed on her. He clearly wanted her to understand what this picture she held meant to him. “Love comes in every shape, size, and configuration in Destiny.”

“Destiny? You mean your hometown?”

“Yes. Our dads were brothers. Our granddads were brothers, too. Even our great-granddads. Sharing a wife isn’t abnormal here. In truth, it is the customary practice.”

She gazed down at the smiling faces of their parents in the photo. “They sure look happy.”

“They were.”

She wasn’t about to ask these cowboys if they planned on the same kind of family as their parents had had. It made sense they would. How could a woman deal with such an arrangement? What about jealousy? She wasn’t sure but couldn’t deny how joyous their three parents had looked in the black-and-white picture.

She set the photo down on the table and turned to Emmett. “When did they die?”

“Twelve years ago. A plane crash took all of them. It also took our friends’ parents. The Knights and the Colemans.”

The air grew thick with the apparent ancient grief of the three cowboys. “You must’ve been only teenagers.”

“I was eighteen and the twins were fifteen. The whole town grieved with us. The O’Learys took all the orphaned teens under their wings. They’re a local wealthy family. They’re like grandparents to us now.”

“It’s not the same as having your own parents.” Her heart ached for them. What a loss at such a young age. “I’m so sorry.”

“It was a long time ago, Amber.” Emmett stood. “We survived. I think you should get back in bed.”

Even though his suggestion was harmless, she felt her cheeks burn as she imagined what it might be like with these three cowboys, her rescuers, surrounding her in a bed. They’d proven they would care for her every need already. Attentive was an understatement.

“Look at her eyes,” Cody said. “She is tired.”

Her eyelids did feel suddenly heavy.

Emmett helped her to her feet. “I insist, Amber. Sleep. We can talk more in the morning.”

“But I have more questions for you guys. Lots more questions.” Before she could continue her argument to remain with them, a long yawn escaped her mouth.

“That’s it.” Emmett lifted her up into his arms. “Bed. Now.”

She placed her forehead into his chest. “Yes, Sir.”

* * * *

Emmett looked at the golden liquid in his glass. Whiskey sometimes was the best medicine, and he sure could use some right now. His body was tired, not ill, but his mind was troubled. Cody was not about to back down when it came to Amber, and that definitely meant trouble. He’d seen him around women many times—at Phase Four, here, and a thousand other places. When Cody was attracted to a female, he was pedal to the metal. But this time was different. His brother was holding back, for him at least. Bryant, too, was acting different around Amber. He didn't want to see them get hurt. Not again.

"You're deep in thought," Cody said, placing his empty glass down on the table.

"Yep."

Bryant knocked back the rest of the contents in his glass.

His gut tightened. Since Amber's arrival, the twins' conduct had troubled him. He was concerned for her, for them, for himself—though the latter wasn't a luxury he could afford. "That's number three for you?"

"Yes it is." Bryant stood. "And it won't be my last."

"You better slow down. We've got to check the roads in the morning."

"You're not one of my dads, Emmett. Stop trying to be. I'm twenty-seven. I don't need a parent."

Bryant didn't normally share so much.

"Okay. Fill your boots for all I care." But he did care. He cared a whole helluva lot. Cody and Bryant were more than brothers to him. He trusted them with his life. He felt responsible for them. Bryant was the quietest of the three of them. Not introverted, so to speak, but definitely a man of few words. Apparently the whiskey and Amber's presence in the other room were having an impact on his tongue and his emotions.

Damn, how could he stop them from falling for Amber? They'd been through so much.

Bryant poured himself another drink, draining the bottle, and sat back down.

They sat in silence around the kitchen table. What were his brothers thinking? He could venture a guess that Cody was working out a plan to seduce Amber. Bryant was a mystery.

"Listen to me. We've got to keep our hands off of Amber," he stated, hoping they would really hear him.

"Why?" Cody asked.

"Don't be an idiot. You saw her. She's gorgeous. A woman like her can't be single. Some guy has a claim on her, mark my words."

"Emmett, you've always been the guy who looks at the glass as half empty. I, on the other hand, see the glass half full. She's here for a reason. We're from Destiny. It's more than a name. She's our future. Fate brought her to us."

What the hell was he talking about? "Fuck, you're out of your mind, Cody. She doesn't even know who she is. She could be anyone."

"I don't give a damn who she is. She's ours. You'll see."

This wasn't going the way he'd hoped. "Bryant, help me out here. Talk to your twin, please. Knock some sense into him before I have to."

Bryant downed half the contents of his glass. "Who knows, Emmett? Maybe Cody is onto something." His brother's eyes were pointed in the direction of Amber, who was asleep in the other room.

"Thank you. He's more than a little interested in Amber, too. I bet if you admit the truth, Emmett, you are, too." Cody grinned broadly.

He didn't like where this discussion was leading. "I won't admit to anything. She's in our care. None of us will make any moves on her. Got it?"

Bryant slammed his glass down on the table. "What does that mean?"

Two against one. Not good. "We're Doms. You know what that means, or have you both forgotten?"

Cody shrugged. "This isn't about the club."

"No, it isn't, but it is about what has worked for us. Just the other day you told me that being a Dom meant something to you."

"Yes, I did." Cody kept his eyes locked on him, though his lovesick armor seemed to be cracking a bit.

"And you," Emmett said, turning to Bryant. "You've insisted we follow protocols to the letter whenever we've trained a sub. Why is that?"

"It's the right thing to do."

"Exactly. The same is true here, guys. Amber may be married. She may have kids." His gut tightened, but he went on. "She might have a life to go back to. Being a Dom matters to me, and I know it matters to you, too. Do I hope she's single and will choose us when her memory returns? Of course. But until then we must abide by protocols. We'll care for her. We'll make sure she's safe. We'll do whatever we need to do to help her fully recover. That's all we do. That's the right thing to do—for her."

"Agreed." Bryant stood up.

"Fuck, I hate this." Cody's hands curled into fists. "We need to lock up the playroom."

"Where's the key?" Bryant asked. "I know we have one, but have we ever had to lock it up before?"

"Never," Emmett answered. "I think I have it on my keychain." He pulled out the set. "Yep. Here it is."

They'd had the playroom built a few years ago. Equipped with a wide assortment of sex toys, a spanking bench, cuffs, and more, they'd used it for private training sessions for new subs. Emmett actually preferred the club for training most of the time.

"I wish the fucking rain would stop. We need to find her car." Cody's tone held a possessive quality that meant the peace would only hold for a short time.

"I hope so, too." What the hell was he going to do if Cody broke ranks and forgot what being a Dom really signified? What about Bryant? His resolve wasn't so certain either. What could he do to force them to make the right choice when it came to Amber?

*Hell, what about me?* Emmett wasn't confident in his own granite, which seemed to crack whenever Amber was near him.

"She's the one," Cody said quietly. "You'll see. I know we've shared women before, but none like her. You have to admit that."

"Even if I do, that doesn't mean she's for us." He'd always expected they would eventually settle down with a woman, likely one of the locals. Amber's arrival had come out of nowhere. He didn't like surprises, preferring to be ever prepared for the unexpected.

"You do like her, don't you?" Cody asked.

"She's quite a woman. What man wouldn't?" Like her? Oh yes, but he was also worried she would rip his heart out and his brothers' when her memories returned. "We really don't know her, Cody."

"I know enough."

"Chill out," Bryant said. "We don't know her. She doesn't know herself. It isn't fair to her to push. Right?"

Cody didn't answer. He picked up the framed photo of their parents Amber had left on the table. The pain in his eyes was familiar to Emmett.

Why had they told Amber about their parents? About what a family meant to them? She'd asked. That was why, but ever since, he couldn't stop imagining her in his and his brothers' bed. A real family. Fuck, he was even imagining raising kids with her.

"Damn this rain." Cody raised his fists up and stared at the ceiling. "Rain or shine, tomorrow I'm looking for her car."

"Deal. Besides, we need to check the road. I'm betting it's blocked." Keeping their minds on work instead of Amber and pie-in-the-sky scenarios was definitely best.

Bryant let out a long, sad sigh. "What if she is married?"

He turned to his brother, who looked more lost than he'd seen him in years. "We'll deal with it as it comes."

"I don't think I can. Maybe it's the whiskey talking, but I'm with Cody on this. Amber certainly feels like the one I could spend the rest of my life with, Emmett. I know it's ridiculous but it's true."

Emmett felt the same way, but he couldn't admit it to his brothers. "I know the ratio of single women in town is low, but there are some. I'm not ready to settle down yet, but when we do, we should choose someone from Destiny, don't you think? Someone who knows our ways? I can think of five attractive dolls who would fit the bill perfectly for us."

"Bullshit." Bryant's tone cut him to the core. "Don't try to sell us a bill of goods, Emmett. I saw how you looked at Amber, how you took care of her. If she's married, it will kill me. It will kill Cody. And you know it will kill you, too."

He nodded. "We still have to keep our cocks in our pants. Things with Amber will either go our way or they won't. I pray Cody is right and fate brought her to us, but we all know how cruel fate can be, don't we?" He didn't wait for either of them to answer. "We're agreed then. Until we know who she is, we follow protocols and are hands off?"

"Agreed," Bryant said.

"Yes," Cody said through clenched teeth. "I agree."

"Great. I'm going to check on Amber. Every couple of hours I will wake her up to make sure she is still okay. Good night." Emmett stood and left his brothers still brooding at the table. He needed to be alone with his thoughts. He'd always thought Cody's romantic nature to be foolish, mocking him at every turn. Now, Emmett's thoughts were running the same route, imagining a forever with Amber, the woman he couldn't get out of his head no matter how hard he tried.

He walked up to the door to the playroom. He opened it and peered in. It was so easy to imagine placing Amber on the spanking bench, seeing her eyes unfocused, her jaw slack, her body pink, all from the pleasure he and his brothers could give her. He felt himself smile at the thought.

Just as fast as the grin had spread out, it turned down into a frown. He was a fool to think things would turn out good for him and his brothers. That didn't happen for them. Strength mattered. That was what had gotten him through many a nightmare.

The pit of his stomach clenched tight. Would this time be different? Would he survive? Would his brothers? Somewhere deep inside, he knew they would not come out of this time with Amber unscathed.

Everything had changed for them since he'd found her in the road. He closed the door to the playroom and put the key in the lock, resolving to keep his guard up. He would make certain that Amber would never see this room.

# Chapter Six

Amber sat on the rocking chair on the front porch of the cabin and watched the three cowboys who had taken her into their home as they saddled two of their horses. Six days and nights of rain had kept them inside, though Cody and Emmett had tried to get down the road a few times. No luck. Every low spot was flooded.

The morning after she'd arrived, Emmett had hiked down to a nearby payphone and called the doctor. He'd given Emmett instructions, which the men had followed exactly. All three cowboys had watched her closely those first couple of days. The care they'd taken with her had touched her heart. Her headache had gone away quickly and she hadn't had any dizziness after that first day. She was going to be okay thanks to her soldier cowboys.

Amber and the guys had been reduced to staying indoors. She'd talked to them about everything. They'd had a great childhood until their parents' accident. Emmett had kissed college good-bye, deciding it was best to keep his brothers together. Quite the sacrifice.

"You going to be okay with Bryant, Amber?" Cody asked. "I think my bedside manner is better than his, don't you agree?"

"I'm not bedridden, cowboy. Go. You have work to do." After so many gloomy days, it felt good to have the sun warming her face.

Emmett jumped on his horse. "You going to check out the south gate, Cody, or will I have to run the entire line by myself?"

Cody glared at him but didn't answer. He got on his horse and tipped his hat toward her. "Sweetheart, don't fret. I'll be back soon."

The tension between those two had grown and grown. She wasn't sure what the problem was, but it was obvious that they were on opposite sides of some issue—likely something to do with her. Cody's blatant flirtations were coming faster and faster as each day passed. Emmett had no interest in her, of that, she was certain. She'd misread him the first couple of days. Unlike Cody, he barely gave her a first glance of late, let alone a second. What had she done to cause such a turnaround in him? She had no idea.

"Be careful," she told them.

"Always, love," Cody answered, but as expected, Emmett didn't say a word.

After learning about them having two dads and the makeup of what a "normal" family for them was, she'd dreamed of what life might be like in such an arrangement. Foolish really, but she couldn't stop playing and replaying the mental movie in her head. All three of the gorgeous men had been so kind to her the first couple of days. Cody continued to charm her. Bryant still seemed to like her, but his quietness kept her guessing what he really thought about her. Emmett was the one that had changed the most. It wasn't what he did that troubled her. He ran her bath every night. He made sure her every request, no matter how small, was met instantly. He insisted she get to bed early. His actions seemed to indicate some level of caring, but other things made her wonder.

As he and Cody rode off in opposite directions, she prayed they would find a car that would have her personal effects in them. According to the brothers, there was no way she could've gotten on their ranch without a car or a horse. The clothes Emmett had found her in didn't seem conducive to riding horseback. A car. That had to be how she'd come. What if the boy that haunted her dreams was in the car? That thought had troubled her more than once over the past few days, but she kept reminding herself that Emmett had found her alone. No one else had been with her.

Bryant sat down next to her. "You okay, Amber?"

"I'm fine," she lied. She didn't want them to know how worried she was.

He grabbed her hand. "You don't have to lie to me."

"Maybe not to you, but to Emmett, I do." She closed her eyes tight, wishing she could take back her words.

"Give him time, sweetheart," Bryant said, squeezing her fingers. "He's dealing the best he knows how."

"I know. You guys have been great. Really. I don't know what I would've done if Emmett hadn't found me." She could have just died there on the road.

"Stop, Amber. He did find you. Cody thinks that it had something to do with fate. I'm beginning to think he may be right."

Of course Cody would think that. Cody saw the world through rose-colored glasses. It was sweet and sexy, but Amber knew the truth. "Emmett doesn't want me. I won't change the future you guys are supposed to have."

"You're wrong, honey." He stroked her hair. "Emmett wants you more than you can possibly imagine. I know him. He's into you bad, but he won't act on that until he's certain about something."

"If I'm married or not, right?" Amber knew Emmett was trying to protect her. She could have kids and a husband out there looking for her right now.

"You got it."

Her head started pounding. Why were her memories so locked away from her? "What kind of person can I be, Bryant? What if whatever I left in the past was horrible? What if I was alone? If I was in love, don't you think I would remember that? Remember some man who held my heart in his hands? It just doesn't make sense to me that I would forget someone like that. My whole life experience available to me is the past week with you, Cody, and Emmett. It's been amazing. I can't even conceive of hitting my head hard enough to jar your images out of my mind."

It had been an incredible week. The guys had taken turns cooking for her those first couple of days. They'd eaten their meals together, talking and laughing the whole time. They'd told her funny stories from their childhood on the ranch. When they'd finally decided she was getting better, they'd let her help in the kitchen. She'd been surprised to know she had some basic cooking skills. She could make a mean grilled cheese.

"Sweetheart, you're worrying too much about this."

"Am I, cowboy? I don't think so. I don't want to remember. Whatever it was must've been horrible. What other explanation is there? Tell me." Why would she have been in the middle of nowhere, alone? It didn't make sense.

"I don't know what to say." Bryant left his chair. "Let's go inside. I'll make you some tea."

Her heart was racing in her chest, making her light-headed. Once Emmett and Cody returned, the dream would be over. She would have to return to reality. What if her memories came back and her tomorrows would be without Bryant, Cody, and Emmett? She couldn't bear the thought. "I'm in the mood for something besides tea." She stood up and stepped right in front of him.

Her initial attraction to the three cowboys had grown and grown until now, it was an uncontrollable desire. She'd gone from being enticed by the three to being unable to shake her need for them. When she'd questioned the locked door across the hall from her room, they'd told her that it was their playroom. The next half hour was spent with them explaining BDSM to her. Emmett had kept trying to change the subject, but Cody hadn't been dissuaded. He'd furthered her curiosity and salacity by spending several evenings telling her about it in more detail. She knew it was a mistake, but all she'd been able to think about since was submitting to the three men.

Bryant's eyebrows shot up. "And what would you be in the mood for, sweetheart?"

"This." She came up on her toes and pressed her mouth to his thick, manly lips. Melting into the kiss was her whole world at the moment. She closed her eyes, enjoying the intimacy with this amazing cowboy. Nothing else mattered. Not her memories. Not her past. Not her future. Now. Here. With Bryant.

She opened her eyes and saw his big orbs staring back at her. She pulled away. "I'm sorry. I shouldn't have done that."

He stroked her hair. "It's all right, baby. It's okay."

"No it isn't. I shouldn't have—"

His lips crashed against hers, silencing her protest. He held the back of her head with his left hand. His right hand feathered her neck as he continued to kiss her.

She shook her head, freeing herself from his devastating kiss that was awakening something deep inside her. "This is stupid. We shouldn't."

He kissed her temple. "You're such a tiny thing, Amber. So sweet. I don't think this is stupid. It's fate. It's our destiny. You were right in saying that if you were in love with someone, you would remember. I believe you. I've never felt this way about anyone before, Amber. You're the one. I've been following Emmett's protocols. No more. I don't care if you do have a past. You're mine. I'm certain of that. You've been mine since you arrived. I know that now. You know it, too. These are the only memories we need. I want to make one with you today. Right or wrong, we have now. Today. This moment. I'm not willing to wait. Understand?"

She hesitated. "What about Emmett? What if you're wrong? What if he isn't interested in me? Won't this head us down a path we need to avoid?"

"Fuck it. I've always been the peacemaker between my two brothers. Emmett, so serious and so cautious. Cody, a complete mess, chasing dreams. I'm done with that. I want the dream. Let them figure out what they want, Amber. I want you. I want you now. I will have you. You can't imagine how hard it's been. I've hungered for you." He scooped her up and carried her into the cabin. "My starvation is about to come to an end. I'm going to drive you mad with pleasure, Amber."

"I would like that, cowboy. Very much." Her whole body

stiffened. What if this was a mistake? A bad mistake? "Bryant, I'm not sure we should."

"You're wrong, sweetheart. We definitely should." His tone was lusty and deep. He meant business.

How could she refuse him? She couldn't, but more than that, she didn't want to refuse him. Her whole body was limp in his arms.

He brought her into the bedroom and lowered her down to the soft quilt below.

"It's not too late for us to think clearly, Bryant. We need to talk."

"No words. I'll talk with my hands." His voice rumbled along the skin on her neck causing her to tremble. He unbuttoned the shirt, a man's shirt, just one of the few she'd worn since arriving. Was it his shirt? Cody's? Emmett's? It didn't matter. She wouldn't be wearing it much longer.

His fingers parted the shirt, and her chest was exposed for him. The bra she'd been wearing when Emmett had found her had been tossed away, its tears beyond repair. His fingers traced her breasts, causing her to shiver. When his thumbs and index fingers clamped down on her nipples, she gasped.

"You like?"

The sting softened into a wave of warmth throughout her body. "Yes. It feels great, but I'm not sure we should keep heading down this path, Bryant."

"You said it yourself, sweetheart." Bryant slipped the oversized jeans down her legs with ease and tossed them aside. "You would've remembered someone by now. I can buy that you might've been in shock at first and forgotten this mystery man, but now, I can't believe you wouldn't have remembered something."

She closed her eyes, and the image of the boy came up. No man. No husband. No boyfriend. No one. Seeing the young kid was all that was left to her. Who was he to her? Where was he? Was he okay? Frustrated tears rolled down her cheeks. "I wish I could remember anything, but I can't." Amber opened her eyes and saw Bryant completely stripped. If she gave in to this muscled cowboy, surrendered to him, what then? Emmett clearly didn't have any interest in her, no matter what Bryant believed. Cody definitely did, and now she knew for certain that Bryant did, too. But that wasn't enough. She'd learned from the first couple of days that these three brothers were meant to share a woman. It was what they'd grown up expecting. She couldn't be the one who divided them up. No way. "I can't do this."

As Bryant's hands removed the shirt completely off her, his mouth came down on hers, forcing her to see another way, another possibility. He was insistent, powerful, and so dangerous. She was falling for him, had been since waking up from her accident. In truth, she was falling for all of the Stone brothers. Bryant had a side to him she hadn't expected. Surprising and exciting. She placed her hands on his chest, thinking she should push him away. Of course he was too strong for her to have any real physical impact, but if he could feel her resistance, she thought he might slow his sensual attack. But her hands felt his rock-solid frame, and she couldn't push away. Instead, she enjoyed the feel of his chest under her fingertips.

It might be smart to stop, to protest, to be logical, but she couldn't. Whatever secrets were lost to her, she wanted this—heaven forgive her—wanted to be with Bryant. She moved her hands around his thick neck and melted into his muscled frame. Bryant was powerful and demanding, but his mouth was gentle and teasing. His tongue slipped across her lips, causing a new set of shivers to ignite inside her. Parting her mouth, she welcomed his tongue. With no memories left to her, this felt like her very first kiss. A real kiss. A kiss for the ages. Bryant was in charge, tugging on her hair ever so slightly. Instinctively, she felt her whole body soften against him. Surrendering to him came so natural to her.

He deepened their kiss, which enkindled sensations zipping like a thousand hummingbirds darting here and there inside her. As he continued claiming her mouth as his, his hands gently massaged her breasts. She knew letting his will mingle with her want, her thirst, her desire, was going to end badly. Once her past life came back to claim her, all she would have left of him would be the image of his face to haunt her for the rest of her days. His face and his brothers'.

He moved his thick, manly lips off her mouth and to her neck, making her tingle violently.

Somehow, she found a shred of logic inside her to latch onto. It wasn't right to go on. He deserved better from her. "Bryant?"

"You're in your head, aren't you, love? Thinking too much, I bet." His words came out in long, deep syllables, making her shiver with every masculine, demanding inflection.

"What if I can't give you what you want?"

"What do you mean?"

Then it hit her like a brick between the eyes. "What if I'm a virgin?" She didn't know.

Bryant stopped caressing her breast. He leaned up and looked at her directly in the eye. "I hadn't thought of that."

She'd hit a nerve in him. "Neither had I, but what if it's true?"

What happened next shocked her. Instead of a frown, the broadest smile came across his handsome face. "That would please me more than you can imagine, Amber. It would mean you are most certainly unattached."

"I can't remember ever having sex, Bryant. What if I don't know how to please you?" Her pulse was pounding hard and fast.

"We'll take things slow, love." He cupped her breasts again with his big hands. "All you have to do is let me take the reins. Your pleasure is my pleasure. I'll know if you're a virgin or not. Either way, I want you. I've wanted you since I first saw you. Once we headed down this path, I had no plans on this being a quickie. Now that I have you where I want you—under me—I'm going to make this last a very long time. Knowing that this might be your first time, I will go especially slow. Stop fighting me. You're mine. Here. Now. Mine."

Without her memories, this felt like her first time. How could she know? The wall kept her from her past, and for now, she was glad of it. “Yes. I’m yours.”

“You’re my sweet virgin princess. Exploring every inch of you will be such a thrill.” He once again kneaded her breasts, causing her nipples to jut out. “I’m going to suck on your gorgeous tits until you are clawing my back.” He pinched her nipples, delivering a sweet sting. “I’ll dine on your beautiful breasts for as long as I like and you will let me. Understand?”

She nodded, feeling her will give way to him. This side of the quiet Stone brother was something she hadn’t expected, but his demands were reaching into her and melting all her impediments, her defiance, her resistance. Even with the butterflies in her belly fluttering wildly, she couldn’t stonewall him any longer. He wanted her, and God help her, she wanted him. Whatever her past, she was swamped with desire.

His mouth came down on her breast and he sucked hard, clamping down on her tip with his teeth every so often. The delicious pain reached down into her pussy, enhancing her sensations, elevating her to another state, a state of dizziness and desire. She squirmed under his assault as liquid seeped out of her pussy.

“Fuck, I could suck on your nipples from sunup to sundown and all through the night. You’re perfection, Amber.”

She didn’t know what to say to that, but felt a big dose of pride swell inside her.

“You’re going to go to the brink of madness, love. I’m going to make sure of it.”

Bryant swallowed her other nipple, delivering the same pleasing sensations he’d done to the other. With his left hand, he continued massaging her breast. Her nipples were aching, so sensitive she had to bite her lower lip to keep from screaming. With his right hand, he slipped his fingers in the waistband of the underwear she was wearing. It wasn’t hard for him to get to her mound, since the briefs were men's, not women's.

"Yes," she blurted out, unable to hold her tongue.

"Time to touch your sweet pussy, Amber. I've been dreaming of this ever since you arrived." His fingertips danced over her mound and then landed on the valley of her sex. As he parted her pussy's lips, her clit began to throb. She shifted her hips so that her pussy pressed into his hand. Even with her memories lost to her, she knew this couldn't be her first time, though it definitely felt like it was. Her mind might not recall sex, but her body most definitely did. Instinct was taking over. She wanted him, wanted his cock inside her pussy. Needed to be filled up and claimed. It would be the only thing to really satisfy this itch he'd awakened inside her.

"Nice and wet for me, love. That pleases me." His fingertips glided over her mound and then pressed on her clit, coating it with her own juices. "I'm going to taste your little button. I'm going to nip at it until you are mad with pleasure."

"Yes. Please." As his talk grew more and more lurid, she felt her want expand and spread out inside her.

"I'm betting your pussy tastes delicious. I love pussy, Amber. I'm going to love drinking all your sweet cream." He shifted down her body, his tongue tracing her flesh like a hot pen.

Down he went, leaving her breasts, arriving at her stomach. She trembled as his lips traced her skin there, causing her temperature to rise to the nearly unbearable.

"Yes," she breathed in a whisper. Her pussy was soaked and her clit was throbbing.

With his tongue bathing her stomach, Bryant worked over her pussy with both his hands. His fingers were like ten caressing masseurs on her pussy and clit. His touches were paradise.

He licked at her navel, which surprised her how sensitive it was. Tingles flooded every part of her body, including deep in her core.

"I'm going to love fucking this tight pussy, sweetheart, filling you up with my cock. I'm going to fuck you out of your mind and then some. I've waited for this, dreamed about this, thirsted for this. No more. Not any longer. You're going to take everything I have to offer. You're going to scream, and it will be music to my ears."

"Oh God." His words were like sensual bullets, piercing her flesh, raising her need higher and higher.

"Time for a taste of your sweet pussy cream." His tongue came out again, dipping below her navel. He moved so slowly, so painfully slow. Down he went with his hot lips. "Look at this luscious clit." He kissed her bud, making her squirm. "Very nice. More on that later, love. Now, I want to drink from your body. You want that, don't you?"

She moved her fingers to his hair, twisting the strands between them. "I do. I need you."

His lips skimmed her clit, causing a spark to shoot up and down her spine until it finally settled in her pussy where it ignited a flame of desire. She nearly screamed when she felt Bryant's tongue move through her swollen, wet pussy.

"Fuck, you taste incredible." His tone was more animal than human, and that brought out a shiver and moan from her. "Now that I've drank your juice, I will have it anytime I want. You will give me drop after sweet drop whenever I command."

She nodded, loving how in control he was. Quiet, no more, Bryant was in charge, not her, and she loved every second of it. No worries existed in this moment. No pain. No wall. She shivered as he went back to drowning her with amazing oral sex.

Bryant held her thighs, parting her legs wider. His fingers clamped around her flesh, locking her in place. Clearly, he wasn't going to let her go, not until he drained her of every splash her pussy produced. She was his to command, to control, to dominate, and knowing that set her free to really feel pleasure. Her body softened as her submission to him was complete. Whatever he wanted from her, she would give over. Whatever he needed, she would surrender.

His thumb pressed on her aching clit, sending her to the roof. A delicious delirium shook her as he lapped up her pussy's liquid like a man mad with thirst.

Her heart pounded hard in her chest. Keeping her body still was impossible now. Her pussy began to spasm, clenching and unclenching over and over. "Please don't stop," she said, panting.

She heard him growl, which made her even wetter, if that was possible. His fingers parted her pussy lips, allowing his tongue to go deeper into her channel. The oral fucking pushed her into a flood of climactic sensations that took her over completely. Hot flames burned her inside and out. Her body was responding with electric pulses that left her ferociously feverish and trembling. Bryant didn't ease up on her as she clawed at his back and screamed his name again and again. His transporting torture continued with his mouth sucking her labia and his fingers squeezing her thighs. Every cell inside her exploded with pleasure and fire.

# Chapter Seven

Bryant looked at Amber's trembling lips and felt his cock pulse hard and his balls grow even heavier. "You're beautiful, love." He moved his gaze to her pillowy-soft breasts. The only word to describe her perfect symmetry was "stunning." Her nipples were still temptingly erect. How could he make her understand how much he loved her breasts? Hell, her whole body was utter perfection. "Get ready for more, sweetheart."

She sucked in a deep breath, clearly attempting to stabilize herself. No way was he going to let that happen. Not yet. Keeping Amber unsteady was critical to get her body and mind in a state of pure pleasure.

He watched her chest rise and fall as her breaths began to soften slightly. "How are you doing, sweetheart?"

She reached down and touched his cheek. "I feel great, cowboy. How about we cuddle now?"

As he moved up her body, he touched her soft skin with his fingertips. "I want that, baby, but not yet. Not until I've fucked your pretty mouth and your delicious tits."

"What if I'm not good at oral sex, Bryant? You were amazing. I'm not sure I can live up to your expectations."

"There you go again, trying to take charge." He cupped her chin and forced her to look at him with her gorgeous eyes. "I'm in control. I will guide you every step. I will teach you. You will do great."

"You think so?" she asked meekly.

"I know so, love." Her submissive nature was so evident. She was the perfect mix of sass and surrender. He could imagine how wonderful it would be to really train her, to take her into the playroom with his brothers, to see her face slack with pleasure and her ass pink and hot from paddles and his open hand. "I want you completely spent, and when you think you can't bear more pleasure, I will fuck your pretty little pussy with my cock."

Bryant opened the drawer in his nightstand and grabbed the bottle of lubricant and a couple of condoms. The rubbers were for later. "Time to feel your tits tighten around my cock." He squirted a generous portion of the slick liquid in the valley between her breasts. Then he began massaging her and was rewarded with her long eyelashes fluttering wildly. "God, you have the most amazing tits, Amber."

Her nipples were hard little points. He rolled them between his thumb and forefinger.

She bit her lip and moaned. He cupped her breasts, enjoying how ample they felt in his hands. "Nice and soft, love. God, I love them."

She smiled. "I believe you do, cowboy."

Her words made his cock strain. He pressed his cock against the opening of her wet pussy and she moved her hips in response.

"Not yet, baby." His own hunger was fathomless, deep, and crushing, but he wanted her to feel pleasure far beyond where he'd taken her so far. His need would have to wait.

"God, I can't stand much more."

"You will, though. Much more." He pinched her nipples harder than before. The moan that slipped past her lips thrilled him. He looked down at her twin mounds, glistening from the lubricant he'd applied. "Time to fuck your pretty titties."

"Please." More like a breath than a word, Amber's nails clawed into the flesh at the back of his neck. "Oh, please, Bryant."

"Talk to me, baby. Tell me what you want. Don't hold back." He moved up her body, positioning himself so that his cock landed between her breasts.

"Anything you want from me, cowboy. That's what I want." The truth in her tone was clear. She was lost to her desires, and he loved that he'd brought her to that place where she could really feel.

He squeezed her tits together around his dick and then slid his rigid erection in and out of the tight spot he created between her breasts. She moved her hands over his, pushing against the back of his hands with her tiny fingers.

Where his past experiences in the playroom and at Phase Four had been primarily fast and effective, today with Amber he wanted it to be unhurried, measured, and deliberate. He wanted it to last. She deserved much more than a quick roll in the hay. She deserved all of him—not just his skill as a trained Dom, not just his ability to fuck a woman into oblivion, not just his talent to deliver mountains of pleasure. No. Amber deserved much more. She deserved all of him.

"Keep talking, Amber. What are you feeling? What do you want?" He tweaked her straining nipples as he continued thrusting between her breasts. "Talk to me."

"God, so much. I don't know how to describe what I'm feeling. I want you, cowboy. I want you inside me."

"I want that more than you can even imagine, and I will fill your pussy up with my dick. I promise. Whatever you want, I'll give it to you."

"Oh, God, that feels so good." Amber moaned.

"You squeeze my dick, baby." He freed his hands from under hers, and she obeyed his instructions, shoving her breasts together even more than he had. "That's my girl." He wove the fingers of his left hand into her thick locks and tugged.

Her eyes closed and her lips vibrated.

With his right hand, he touched her cheek. "You're fucking unbelievable, love."

The scent of her arousal grew. He inhaled her aroma deep into his nostrils, and his hunger expanded. He'd been known to come more than once in a night, but today he planned on coming at least three times—even if it took all day. That wouldn't be bad, not at all.

"I can smell how wet your pussy is, Amber. I'm going to come on you here, baby. I'm going to feed my cock to your sweet little mouth. Then, when you think I'm done, when you think you can't bear one more second of pleasure, I'm going to shove my cock into that tight, pretty pussy and fill you up completely. Understand?"

"Oh God, this is too much already."

"Not even close, love." He tugged a little harder on her hair, and she whimpered deliciously. Then she compacted his cock between her tits even more, tightening her hands together. "Perfect, Amber."

He was so close to shooting his seed between her tits and onto her neck and face. The hot pulse in his veins sped up. "Close. So close."

"Do it, cowboy. Please."

"Fuck, yeah." Every muscle in his body tightened, and he shoved his hips forward. His seed shot out of his dick in a thick white stream, covering her gorgeous face and neck with pools of his cum.

"Bryant?" She was writhing under him like a live wire.

He didn't move positions but stroked her face. "Yes, love?"

"Do you know how much this means to me? Being with you this way?"

Her sweet words reached deep into him. "Yeah, baby. I think I do."

She smiled and wiggled her hips under him.

His cock responded, straining back to a full erection. He shifted down until they were once again face-to-face. "I think you need a big, hard cock inside you."

She grinned and nodded.

He kissed her and shoved his index finger into her pussy. She moaned into his mouth.

"Well, look at how you two decided to fill up the time while I was gone. Very nice. I think I'll join you before Emmett comes back."

Bryant turned to the doorway and saw Cody smiling his approval and stripping off his shirt.

* * * *

With Cody's sudden appearance, Amber trembled violently under Bryant. "Why are you back so quick?"

"The road got too treacherous for me and Tux."

She had come to love all the guys' horses. Tuxedo was Cody's. "How bad is it?" she asked, hoping to keep him talking while she could figure a way out of this embarrassing mess.

"It's mucked up really bad. It'll take several days of sun to dry it out enough before I take him out again." He removed his boots and placed them in the corner. Standing with only his Levi's on, Cody smiled at her. "Now, let's have some fun, shall we?"

"Please, guys, this seems so fast."

"Pet, you've been here almost a week. This isn't fast at all." Cody took off his jeans, and she could see he wasn't wearing underwear. Of course he was going commando. In the short time she'd known him, how could she expect anything else? Without thinking, she glanced down his ripped body and shredded abs until her gaze landed on his dick. It was long and thick, an exact replica of Bryant's cock. The two were physically identical in every way, mirror images of one another.

Cody took a couple of steps to the bed, and she closed her eyes. "What if Emmett comes back now? You did. Won't the road the direction he went be just as bad?"

"No, pet," the insistent twin said. "It's much rockier on the north road. He won't be back until dark. Besides, if he does show, then he'll see I've been right about you all along."

So the tension between them had been about her. "Right about me? What do you mean?"

"You're ours, Amber. I believe in fate. Things don't just happen. There's a purpose, a destiny."

Destiny. It did seem that it was her destiny to end up here, with these three incredible men. "Does that mean you think I'm meant for you and your brothers?"

Cody nodded. "Absolutely. Emmett is stubborn, but he's into you."

"I don't think so." She thought about how he'd stiffened and been so distant with her after the first twenty-four hours she'd been in the cabin. He wasn't mean, but he certainly was not warm. "I'm not sure about this. We've got to be smart. I don't believe Emmett wants me."

Bryant's finger was still inside her pussy and he added another finger to it, stretching her out even more. "Our big brother will come around. You'll see. I'm not letting you go, Amber. Cody's been right all along. Fate brought you to us. Fate will keep you here." He pulled his fingers from her channel. "Nice and wet. Very nice indeed."

Cody crawled into the bed behind her. He cupped her bottom, then parted her cheeks.

The shock of his sudden appearance and the realization of what she thought he planned to do to her made her anxiety shoot up.

"You can't mean to fuck my ass, can you?"

Cody touched her anus with his fingertips. "I'm just playing right now. But eventually we will want to."

Bryant cupped her chin and forced her to turn her head his direction. "When the time comes, you'll love it, Amber. I promise."

With each of Brandon's syllables and each of his and Cody's intimate caresses on her pussy and ass, her body burned hotter and hotter. Her logical side shuffled back into a corner of her mind, silenced by their joint touches. They were in no hurry, clearly taking pleasure in keeping her unsettled and scrambling.

Bryant kissed her, and she welcomed his tongue. Ménage love was their normal. They'd grown up in a loving family with one mom and two dads. Amber didn't have a clue what her normal had been before, but to her this moment with these two cowboys felt right, felt desirable, felt ideal even.

"I hope you're a virgin back here, pet." Cody kissed her on the back of the neck.

Bryant captured her mouth with his, deeper this time, causing her toes to curl. He threaded his fingers in her hair and tugged. With his other hand, he cupped her breast and gently squeezed. All the while, Cody was using his fingers on her pussy, clit, and anus, taking her breath away.

She got even wetter than she'd thought possible.

Cody took the bottle of lube Bryant had gotten from his nightstand a little bit ago and applied a generous amount to his fingers. "Take a deep breath, baby."

She did.

"Let it out." He pierced her ass with his index finger. The initial stretching pain made her squeal.

Bryant kissed her belly lightly.

"You're definitely still a virgin back here, Amber." Cody's lusty tones made her even wetter.

"How do you know?"

Bryant clamped down on her nipple with his teeth, conveying a sweet sting. The strain in her ass from Cody's finger assault and in her nipple from Bryant's bite morphed into a feverish tremble which released a flood of sensations inside her, hot and electric.

"Because it's so tight." Cody's fiery breath danced over her skin like lava. "I can't wait to fuck your sweet ass someday. You'll feel my cock so deep in your ass. You'll know that your ass is mine until the end of time."

Bryant licked her aching nipples until she thought she might go mad. "I'm going to shove my cock inside your pretty pussy, Amber."

"Oh God." No memory of sex came to her. This, for all practical purposes, was her first time—and what a first time it was. Shivering like a leaf in a gust, she fisted the sheets, hoping to hold on for the ride of her life and surrendering both her mind and her body to these two men, these two cowboys—her cowboys.

Bryant sat up, his hot stare searing her inside and out. "Condoms are on my nightstand."

"Why should we?" Cody asked. "She's ours."

"No," she said. "You can't mean to…to—"

"Cody, not this time," Bryant stated flatly.

What did he mean by "not this time?" Before she could get her head around that thought, Bryant smashed his manly lips to her mouth.

"He's right. Not now. I agree. Relax. It's okay." Cody nodded.

Bryant grabbed one of the foil packets. He ripped it open and took out the rubber.

"Thank you," she sighed. "Let me help with this." She took the rubber from him and touched the tip of his cock. A drop of his pre-cum slickened her shaky fingertips. She took a deep breath and rolled the condom down his shaft.

"I've got to get inside you, baby," Bryant said. He rolled on top of her and impaled her with his cock.

She gasped and closed her eyes, feeling his thickness stretch her pussy wide. She couldn't speak, yet her whimpers vibrated deep in her throat. She opened her eyes and gazed into Bryant's eyes, wide with lust and hunger. One of his hands tugged on her hair, reminding her that he meant to control her, to dominate her. His other hand massaged her breast, creating a new flood of sensations. His caresses on her breasts were unlike the pulls on her locks. Those touches were gentle and slow, suggesting another side of him, loving and kind.

"Fuck, you're nice and tight, Amber." The low rumble in his voice made her tremble.

Was this her first time? She wasn't sure. His cock felt enormous inside her, coming so close to painful. But the pain wasn't intolerable and was morphing into something more, pure unabashed desire.

Bryant thrust his dick into her a few times, in and out. "God, your pussy feels so good."

"Roll our baby over so that I can really get a good look at her beautifully rounded ass." Cody's tone was full of sensuality that made her skin tingle.

Bryant's tone was clearly heavy with hunger. "You got it. You let me do the work, pet, understand?"

"Okay."

In a flash, he rolled onto his back, keeping his cock seated deep inside her, pulling her body with his as easy as could be, making her feel even tinier and lighter.

"Oh, God. I'm nervous about this, guys," she confessed shakily.

"Trust us, baby," Bryant said.

Cody rubbed her ass with both his hands. "You're going to love this as much as we are. Maybe more. I promise. But we're not going all the way with this right now."

"You're not?" she asked, surprised and yet relieved. She wasn't prepared to submit to anal sex.

Bryant shook his head and smiled. "For that most intimate act, we will wait for Emmett."

"What if he isn't interested in me that way?" she asked, fearing it might be true.

"He is," Bryant and Cody answered in unison.

Her nipples and clit seemed to be connected by some electrified lines, running up and down her torso in a sensual positive charge.

Cody jumped out of the bed, his cock straight up and swinging slightly from side to side, reminding her oddly of a pendulum. But pendulums weren't so thick, long, or topped with a drop of pre-cum. "Back in a sec."

Bryant touched her clit with his index finger, increasing her already-too-powerful want. His kisses went from her neck to her mouth to her shoulders and back again to her neck.

As promised, Cody returned, holding a sex toy in one hand. "This will come in handy for our sweet Amber." Her grabbed a bottle of lubricant and applied it to the plaything. *Plaything?* It looked too big to her for where he obviously intended to put it—inside her ass.

"Let's get back to pleasuring you, pet." Of all three Stone brothers, Cody was the cockiest, but she didn't find it off-putting at all. Instead, it made her want him all the more.

"You're killing me. Please, kiss me, Cody." They were driving her crazy.

Cody smiled. "We're going to have to make you understand who is in charge, doll."

"Baby steps," Bryant said.

"You'll spoil her, bro," Cody warned. "I'll have to keep an eye on you."

Bryant rolled his eyes. "Ditto here for you. You're the one who is insisting on pleasuring her from behind, not me."

"Guilty."

"What's the plan?"

They had a plan?

"A plug. After seeing her ass front and center, I can't resist." Cody's fingers began circling her anus, drawing out more moans from her lips than before. "Maybe this is a big baby step but it's still a baby step."

"I can't blame you, but I want to get off on the right foot with this pretty little sub." Bryant pinched her nipple, and the sting made her even wetter. "Do you know what you did wrong, baby?"

"No." The fresh sting on the tips of her breasts shot down into her pussy and clit. Both were throbbing and aching. Her breaths came faster and faster, and still she felt like she needed more air in her lungs.

"You tried to take over and run this show when you asked Cody to kiss you." Bryant released her nipples, and the throbbing there and down below intensified to a low burn. "There will be times when you can ask us for something, but only after we give you permission."

"She doesn't know about protocols, Bryant." Cody shoved his fingers into her ass, stretching her even wider than before. The pain was gone, replaced by something new, something powerful. Want. Real, deep, abiding want.

Bryant's eyes never released their hold on hers. "We're not paddling her ass. We reading her signals perfectly and you know it."

She agreed with him. Bryant pressed his hips up, his cock finding a particularly sensitive spot in her pussy. Together with Cody's fingers in her ass, she was so full. They took turns, pulling out while the other plunged in. They were playing her body like an instrument, drawing out new sensual notes with each passing measure. High and sharp. Low and vibrating. Fast. Slow. Up. Down. The music they were creating inside her had her pussy clenching and unclenching again and again.

Cody's lips feathered against her ear. "Listen to me, Amber. I'm going to shove a plug inside your ass. Protocols are simple."

"Now?" Bryant snapped. "You want to give her protocols now?"

"Shut up," Cody continued. "Yes. Now. Amber, you can stop us should we push you past a boundary that is firm inside you."

She struggled to concentrate. "I can?"

"Yes. Three words are all you need to know." Cody scissored his fingers inside her ass. "It's simple. 'Green' means 'go.' 'Yellow' means 'slow.' 'Red' means 'stop.' Got it?"

She nodded but knew that she would never say "red" now. These two cowboys had her deliciously dizzy and ready for whatever they wanted from her. Even now, she couldn't wait to feel Cody replace his fingers with the toy, though it was a little daunting to her logical side.

"Let's test her," Cody said in a deep rumble. "What state are you in, sub?"

She rubbed her thighs together, tightening her pussy around Bryant's dick. "Green. I'm green."

"Add a 'Sir' to your responses, pet. That will please us very much."

"Yes, Sir."

"Satisfied?" Bryant asked his twin.

"Yes. Time to enjoy your sweet ass, love." Cody's quiver-inducing caresses up and down her back made her pussy tighten even more. "I'm going to cover your back with my cum."

She looked over at him fisting his cock with one hand.

He smiled, holding the plug with his other hand for her to see clearly. "You ready for this toy, pet?"

As terrifying as the thing looked, she managed a nod.

He slapped her ass, discharging a sizzling bite. "Aloud, sub. Give me your state by color?"

"Yes, Sir. I'm ready. I'm green, Sir."

"Listen to her, Bryant. She's perfect." Cody kissed the back of her head, speaking so slowly that each syllable somehow reached down and caressed her clit. "A natural submissive. I can't wait to strip her of all her worries, her preconceptions. How fun it's going to be to place her on the spanking bench and run our hands over this sweet ass. God, I can't wait to see her flesh grow pink and to hear her moans of ecstasy."

Bryant nibbled on her shoulder. "She is perfect. More than perfect."

Cody's fingers pierced her again. "Sub, you know this ass is mine, not yours. It's mine. Understand?"

She swallowed hard. "Yes, Sir. It's yours. Not mine."

"You want me inside this ass, don't you?"

She wanted it so much, she felt like she was about to die. "Please. Yes, Sir. Green, Sir. I'm green."

"Fuck, you're too much, baby." His words came out more like a low roar than syllables.

Knowing she was taking a risk but unable to hold back, she ventured a request. "Please fill me up, Sir. Take me." The words spilled from her with ease. She wanted them both inside her, making her know from now until forever she was theirs.

Bryant smiled, a hot smile, his eyes capturing her utterly. "Fuck, you feel good, Amber." He gripped her hips, pushing his cock deeper into her wet heat. He stretched her even more, so wide she felt like she might rip in two.

Cody placed the tip of the toy to her anus and pressed. "Take a deep breath, love, and hold it until I say let go."

She obeyed, filling her lungs to the max.

"Hold it. Hold it. Now. Blow it all out."

She parted her lips and emptied all the air inside her. When the last ounce of oxygen was gone, she felt Cody stab her ass with the plug, shoving it all the way in.

She gulped in a roomful of air, fighting the intense shock and biting pain. Her entire body blazed hot and her pussy and ass convulsed fiercely around Bryant's cock and Cody's toy, stretching her insides to the very zenith of possibility.

"Fuck, she's squeezing my dick. Feels so good." Bryant feathered his lips on her, his hot breath warming her face.

Cody brushed her ass with his fingertips, tapping the part of the thing in her ass that was still exposed, delivering a delicious jolt through her body. Each were whispering words of comfort. *It's okay. Just breathe, love. You're doing great. Take your time.*

She wasn't sure who was saying what, but their tenderness and guidance was having an impact. Soon, her breathing softened a bit, and a million staggering sensations were shooting through her body.

"How are you, love?" Bryant asked in the gentlest of tones.

"Green, Sir. I'm all green." To emphasize the point, she clenched her lower half, tightening her pussy around his dick and her ass around Cody's toy.

"Holy fuck, woman. You're asking for it." Cody laughed like a man lost to his own passion. Any civility inside him was gone, and in its place was nothing but a caveman's lust. His taps on the toy came faster and faster, making her dizzy and hot.

Bryant didn't say another word, but his growls and narrowed eyelids made her even wetter. He impaled her pussy with his dick again and again, deeper and deeper. Her cowboys seemed to be enjoying her responses. Every pant from her was rewarded with harder strokes and grunts from them. They knew her better than she knew herself. Each touch took her higher. Each caress burned hotter.

What woman wouldn't surrender to these two?

She clawed at Bryant's chest and cried out as her clit throbbed and her pussy and ass vibrated around his cock and Cody's plug drilling her insides. Her entire body began to shake from the fast-approaching climax.

"Fuck, you're so tight, baby." Bryant shifted her legs wider with his knees, allowing his cock to extend even farther into her pussy.

Cody's toy also stretched her ass even more.

A wave of shattering tingles raced through her. Every inch of her was moving. Her body was in control now, not her mind, not her logic. The friction on her clit from Bryant's body sent her over the edge. She screamed as the explosive orgasm seared her with throbbing, sizzling sensations.

Whimpers poured out of her, matching their dual attacks inside her pussy and ass. Her toes curled so tight, she could almost imagine they could bend steel. Liquid poured out of her pussy, drenching Bryant's cock and her thighs.

"Fuck. I'm going to come." Bryant's eyes closed tight. He shoved his cock all the way in her pussy. Her channel's inner muscles clenched hard around his shaft. "Yes. That's it, baby. Squeeze my dick with your pussy."

She could feel the heavy pulse of his cock as he spilled his seed.

"Color, sub?" Cody ordered in a tone that told her he was close.

Though she was having trouble getting enough air, she managed to speak. "Green, Sir. Green. Green. Green."

"Fuck yeah," he exclaimed. It sounded like a victory cry. And she felt his hot liquid hit her back like lava, bringing another wave of overwhelming sensations inside her body.

Like a wild animal with no self-control, she shifted back and forth between her cowboys, clamping on Bryant's cock and Cody's plug with utter abandon, reaching that spot inside her pussy, enjoying the sweet ripples shooting through her body. Again, she screamed as a fresh hot wave swamped her with pleasure so sharp, so overwhelming, she believed passing out was a real possibility. But she didn't. Instead, she felt her lips tremble as breathless moans left her body. Her mind spun, lost and smothered by the myriad of sensations zipping through her insides. This went on for some time until she became aware of the four hands caressing her, one set on her shoulders, the other on her back. So soft and delicious. Bryant held his cock deep inside her but no longer thrust into her. Cody left the toy in her ass but no longer tapped it. Both were caressing her gently with their large hands.

She listened to their breathing, which was almost as labored as hers. Conscious to a point, she let her mind drift in the haze of the afterglow of pleasure these two cowboys had given her. Even though her whole memories amounted to only a week, it was all that mattered to her now. She'd tried so hard to recall her past to no avail.

Without a word, Bryant shifted his body and hers until they were on their sides. Cody moved closer in behind her. His cock pressed against her ass. What would it feel like to have him inside her instead of the plug? She wanted to find out someday. She was between Bryant and Cody and loving it. She looked into Bryant's beautiful eyes and couldn't imagine a life without him. She felt Cody's fingertips on her lower back and let herself dream of a future with them.

She was so tired of trying to break down the invisible wall that held her memories captive from her. She was tired of being afraid. Whatever she'd left in the past, she was happy to let it stay there. This cabin was her entire life. Here. Only here. These were her men. Her future. Both of them believed Emmett did want her. Could she make him understand that she didn't want to go back to the past, that he and his brothers were her entire world? Somehow she must. She'd fallen in love with Cody and Bryant, but Emmett, too.

He was the kind of man any woman could depend on. He'd come to her rescue full on, with no hesitation. Early on, she'd seen his kindness and strength. Sure, he'd put up his guard around her later on.

Would he bring that down once he heard she was ready to be with him and his brothers, ready to let go of whatever past she'd left? She prayed so.

She needed all of them, including Emmett. She wasn't about to settle for less. Besides, ever since learning how they had grown up and the future they'd expected of sharing a single woman, she wasn't about to come between them. If Emmett really did want her, then she could have her dream. If not, then she would leave. No way would she come between these amazing brothers.

"What the fuck is this?" The voice was one she knew instantly—Emmett's.

She looked at him, his face storming with darkness. Before she could try to make him understand, he stepped into the hallway, slamming the door behind him.

# Chapter Eight

Emmett cursed his cock, which seemed to have a mind of its own after seeing Amber's naked body between his brothers. He didn't bother to get a glass out of the cupboard, but took a long gulp straight from the whiskey bottle he'd found on the counter.

This was a totally fucked-up mess. Cody's actions didn't surprise him, but Bryant's did.

"Fuck," he said aloud. What the hell was he to do now? His cock had its own idea, but he knew that was insane at the very best, at the worst, utter catastrophe.

Bryant came out of the bedroom, fully dressed. He didn't say a word, which didn't surprise Emmett. Their mom had dubbed each of them by a quality that ended up following them into adulthood.

Bryant's was "thinker."

Cody's was "dreamer."

She'd always called him "the judge." It made sense. Looking at all the facts, he knew what his brothers had done with Amber was a mistake. It would end badly for all of them, no doubt about it. Time to swing the gavel and issue punishment. *Fuck.*

Bryant placed an empty glass in front of Emmett and one in front of himself. "We may be ranchers, Emmett, which might mean we aren't the most civilized, but we do have glasses."

"Fuck off." He tipped the bottle up and took another drag of the liquor. It burned his throat all the way down.

"Okay. That's how you're going to play this. Your call."

"Apparently not. We all agreed to keep our dicks in our pants around Amber until we knew her full story. What happened to that,

Bryant? Did Cody trick you somehow into forgetting that promise?"

Bryant stood up and brought out another bottle of whiskey. He sat down, opened the bottle, and filled his glass. He drank down half the contents and then set the glass back on the table.

Cody, wearing only his Levi's, emerged from the hallway.

His brother's infuriating smile pissed off Emmett to no end. He tipped up his bottle and let a big portion of the whiskey coat his throat. The liquor hadn't taken the edge off, and God knew it needed to be softened or he might punch his brothers into the floor until they understood how bad they'd fucked things up.

"So we're drinking." Cody took the bottle Bryant had brought to the table and filled the other glass. "Works for me."

"Where's Amber?" Emmett felt his pulse in his temples, pounding away like a heavy sledgehammer.

Cody drank from his glass. He stared directly at him, as if daring him to start anything. "She's in the bathroom. Said she needed a minute to herself."

"What the fuck were you two thinking? She might be married, or have you both lost your minds? Of course you have. What other explanation could there be for you to take her to bed?" The words burned like acid in his mouth. He was angry with them, most definitely, but he was also afraid for them. Their actions had made them vulnerable again, vulnerable for more pain, more heartache. They didn't deserve that, not after all they'd suffered, no matter how foolish they'd been.

Cody shook his head. "Emmett, why did you come back so quickly? If you had stayed on task, you wouldn't have seen a thing."

"You would've liked that, I bet. One of my stirrups broke. I came back to fix it and found you. Why are you back already? Was that your plan all along, Cody? Get me out of the cabin so you could trick Bryant into taking Amber to bed?"

"Fuck off," Cody snarled. "You're not my dad."

Bryant rolled his eyes. "He came back because the road was

mucked up, Emmett. You know how the south part of the ranch is. And he didn't trick me into Amber's bed. I was already making love to her when he got back."

What was wrong with his brothers? Did their cocks suddenly take control of their brains? "What the fuck were you thinking? Bryant, that's not like you."

Bryant looked up at the ceiling and sighed. "I've been the peacemaker my whole life. You and Cody lock horns again and again. I'm done with it. Amber is my priority from now on." He grabbed the glass and drained the remaining contents into his mouth. Then he poured himself another.

They clearly weren't thinking this all the way through. "You're both fucked. You can't play with Amber's life like that. She's a person, not a plaything. You want to fuck someone, go to Phase Four. There are plenty of subs more than willing to bed either one of you or both, but not Amber. Can't you see what a mess you've made?"

"Stop trying to protect us, Emmett." Cody swirled the liquor in his glass. "We're grown. You mean the world to me, to Bryant. But you have to stop playing parent. Okay?"

"It's not just about you two. What about Amber? What about the life she left behind? The people she left behind."

"What if there aren't any people in my past, Emmett?" Amber stepped from the hallway. She was wrapped up in one of his mother's robes. Where she'd found it, he wasn't sure, but it fit her perfectly. In no way did it remind him of his mother. Instead, Amber's ample breasts made his cock stir again in his jeans.

"We can't know either way," he answered. "That's the point. Until we do know, these two idiots should have kept their hands off of you. Can't you see that?"

She sat down beside him and placed her tiny hand on top of his. "No. I don't see it that way. It's been many days. I believe that if I had someone in my life, someone special, at least one or two memories would've come back about him. None has. Do you see where I'm going with this?"

"Yes. Of course." He turned and faced her directly. God, she was stunningly beautiful. How could he blame his brothers for taking her to bed? He couldn't. They were only human, as was he. But he had to be better, to do better, for them and for Amber. "But none of us are doctors. They might be able to help you remember something."

"I might be a doctor. How can we know?"

"Maybe, but it doesn't matter, sweetheart. You have a past. Whatever it is will be coming for you. A mother or father. A sister or brother. And yes, maybe even a husband." She winced at his last word, which killed him, but he knew he had to go on, to make her and his brothers understand. There might be no way of taking back what had happened between them, but they didn't have to continue down this path of destruction. "You might even have children, Amber. What about them? What about that boy you do remember? Maybe you don't remember everything, but you do remember him."

She closed her eyes and let out a long, worried sigh. He was reaching her.

"Damn it, Emmett. Cool it." Cody's tone was hot, but he couldn't let it dissuade him.

He hated making her come to her senses, making them all come to their senses, but he must. Sure, he would love to grab her up in his arms and take her back to bed and have his way with her. But what would that get him? Pain. A heart ripped to shreds. No. He had to be smart. For her. For Cody. For Bryant. And yes, for himself.

"I can't imagine how hard it is not to know who you are, where you came from, Amber. It's a load I wish I could carry for you. But you do have a past. Likely there are people worried sick that you are missing. All I'm asking is for you to wait until we know more. I blame them." He pointed to Cody and Bryant. "They're good men but they gave in to their urges. They know better."

"I'm glad they did," she said. "You're right about one thing, Emmett. This has been hard, unbelievably hard."

He saw the tears well up in her eyes and his gut clenched. God, how he wanted to hold her, to tell her everything would be okay, but he couldn't. It wouldn't be right.

"Amber, you have to understand."

"No. You have to understand, cowboy. My only memories are of this cabin, of you and your brothers. That's my entire life right now. Even my name feels real to me now. Amber. You and your brothers named me. It's my name. Why am I here in rural Colorado? Why don't I remember what brought me here? Why don't I remember my past, my family, my life? There's something back there so horrible my subconscious has locked it away." Her words were coming fast, filled with obvious panic. She was clearly trying to convince him to change his mind. "You say I might be married. What if I was? It doesn't matter now. If I was in love, do you think a bang to the head would make me forget? I don't. Cody says I'm here because of fate. What if he's right? Can't you see that there is a chance he could be?"

She was shaking violently. Bryant and Cody stood up, making a move toward her.

"Wait." He pulled her into his body and squeezed. "It's going to be okay, Amber. You'll see. We just have to do this the right way. Maybe Cody is right, but we don't know for sure."

She leaned into him and began to sob. "Emmett, aren't you interested in me? Don't you want me to stay here with you?"

He cupped her chin and tilted her face up. "Look at me, sweetheart."

She obeyed, her eyes blinking with heavy tears.

"Amber, you've been through hell. You have to trust me on this. I pray Cody is right. I really do. I want him to be right about you being unattached and meant for us. I've never wanted anything more in my entire life, but none of us knows that's true. We can hope. We can pray. But we don't know. Understand?"

"What if I never know? What then? You can't imagine how hard it is not to know who you are. Sometimes I hope I never remember.

I'm afraid of what might be."

"Listen to me. We are going to find out everything we can." He didn't look away from her. "Cody, we've got to find her car, agreed? I'm sure it's somewhere on or near the ranch. I know it will be hard to locate it with the roads the way they are, but are you willing to go with me to look?"

"Yes. Even if we have to go on foot, we will find her car."

"I'll stay here with Amber," Bryant said.

That hadn't worked out so well this morning. "On second thought, not a good idea. Bryant, you should go with Cody. I'll stay here with Amber," he said.

"A very good idea, Emmett. I fucked up. I see that now." Bryant's voice was replete with regret. "I've proven I'm not trustworthy alone with Amber. You stay with her."

"Bryant, please don't say that," she whispered.

"Sweetheart, this isn't your fault. It's all mine."

"And mine," Cody added.

"I wanted you both. Please don't take away the most amazing memory I have."

Bryant moved beside her and leaned down and kissed her cheek. "I won't, love. Right or wrong, it happened. But Emmett is right. We must figure out who you are. Until then, we have to resist temptation, no matter how difficult it is. That's why I'm going with Cody. I need to clear my head, not just for me, love, but for you, too. It's for the best."

She closed her eyes and nodded her agreement.

Cody came up to her other side. "I still believe in fate, Amber, but I'm willing to wait until we have proof." The earlier certainty in his tone was muted. Clearly Cody knew this might end badly for all of them, but he was willing to find out the truth about her because she so plainly needed to know.

"I'm terrified, guys. What if I've done something awful? I'm not sure finding out who I really am is a great idea."

"Sweetheart," he said softly, hoping to quell her fears. "It's going to be okay. You may be scared but deep down you want to know the truth. Right?"

"Yes. I suppose so."

"They'll go look for your car. When they find it, I'm sure they'll also find your identification inside. Once we know your real name, I'm betting it will jog your memory free."

"I thought it was too difficult for the horses to trek out there."

"Only to the south, sweetheart. If need be, they can set out on foot that direction," Emmett said.

Bryant stroked her hair. Clearly he was gone for her as much as Cody was. Hell, as much as Emmett was, too. "He's right, love. You need to know and so do we. Don't fret. This is going to work out."

"But what if it doesn't? What if the past I've forgotten comes crashing in on us, destroying any chance of…us having…" Amber blinked several times as if trying to find the right words. "I just don't want this to end. Can you understand that, Emmett?"

"I understand more than you can even imagine. Just because we might not like what Bryant and Cody find doesn't mean we should avoid it. Whatever you left, we'll deal with it. Together. Trust me."

She closed her eyes and nodded. "Okay. I will trust you."

# Chapter Nine

Amber finished packing up the basket she'd found under the sink with sandwiches and fruit. Cody and Bryant had returned the night before with nothing to report of their search, which had troubled her and the three Stone brothers. The rains had caused a rockslide that the twins couldn't get past. This morning they'd packed up some camping gear, vowing not to return until they had exhausted all efforts to get around the debris and to find something that would help them discover Amber's real identity. They even said they might ride all the way to town, if they could find a way around the blockage in the road, to talk to the sheriff if their search came up empty. That could mean at least another day, maybe two, before they returned.

"What's this?" Emmett said, returning from brushing down his horse.

"I'm tired of just wringing my hands and waiting. I need to get out and see more than these cabin walls. I made us a picnic lunch."

"And what makes you think I am willing to take you away from here, missy?"

She laughed. He'd been pacing the floor ever since the big discussion around the kitchen table yesterday. "You're as stir-crazy as I am."

"What about the roads? Did you think of that?"

"We don't have to go far, cowboy. Surely there's some place on this ranch we can get to without much trouble."

His manly lips turned up into the sexiest smile. "I can think of one, Amber. I would love to show it to you, too. I think you'd like the view."

She'd thought it would be more difficult to convince him to take her out for lunch. "Let's go."

"I'll have to saddle up Bullet first. I'll be back in a flash."

"Sounds terrific."

The big, muscled cowboy walked back out the door, heading to the barn.

Learning Emmett was truly interested in her had lifted her spirits some. Still, until more was known about her past, her worries remained. His demeanor had softened much since the big discussion, but he still kept himself reticent around her. He'd made it clear that the right thing to do was wait.

She knew he was right but hated it. She still couldn't believe that behind the wall in her mind was a man who was the love of her life. It just wasn't possible. Love wasn't a stranger to her any longer. She'd fallen for Bryant, Cody, and yes, even Emmett.

She set the picnic basket down on the kitchen table and walked to the shelf where she'd placed the wedding photo of her cowboys' parents. Gazing at Mrs. Stone and her two grooms had become a frequent practice for her whenever she was alone. She'd studied the woman's face and could almost feel her utter joy and overwhelming contentment. The dads, too, were totally in love with her.

She closed her eyes and dreamed of a future with the Stone brothers, her cowboys. How would such an arrangement work? What would be the everyday ins and outs of a poly family? She wasn't certain. Still, if the three in the photo could figure out how to live and be happy, she and her three cowboys could do the same.

An image of her standing in a white gown with Cody, Bryant, and Emmett surrounding her floated in her mind's eye. Her heart leapt up in her chest. This was real. This was her life. This was her future. She loved her three rescuers. Real love. Total and unfaltering.

No. There could be no man in her past. It just wasn't possible.

Emmett returned. "Ready?"

She picked up the basket. "I am."

* * * *

Emmett finished another of Amber's sandwiches. Who would've thought to put sliced bananas in a peanut butter and jelly sandwich? Not him. Not the twins.

He couldn't stop staring at her, lit by the late-afternoon sun. She glowed like an angel. Her hair was tied back in a ponytail. Though she looked ravishing no matter how she wore it, he preferred her locks down, falling past her shoulders.

"This is a beautiful place." Amber's voice was as warm and fresh as the breeze they were enjoying. "Thank you for bringing me here."

"I've loved this spot since I was a kid." He pointed to Blue Arrow Peak. "I can stare at that mountain for hours and never tire of it."

"Does it always have snow on it?"

He nodded. "I remember convincing Cody and Bryant when they were little that Bigfoot lived up there. Cody, to this very day, still vows that he's actually seen footprints of the beast."

"I can imagine he does. He's a real believer in a lot of things." A sad looked crossed her face. He knew she was thinking about Cody and Bryant and what they might find.

So was he. "I know how worried you are. I can see it in your eyes. We are going to take care of you, Amber. Understand?"

"Yes, Sir. I'm green, Sir." She snapped out the safe word like a challenge. "Very green, Sir."

He knew she wasn't, of course.

God, how had it come to this? His heart was on the line, and so were his brothers'. Hers, too.

He wanted to believe in Cody's truth, that Amber had come to them as a part of providence, a part of fate. If he had his brother's same conviction, Emmett would've suggested they leave well enough alone and forget trying to find out more about Amber's past. They could've kept Amber's presence secret for quite some time should they have chosen that path. But he didn't have Cody's faith. He'd convinced his brothers and Amber to head down the path of his making. A path that was certain to end badly for all of them. But it was the right thing to do, and he, like always, would do what needed to be done.

She sighed and leaned back on her elbows, causing her ample breasts to be even more pronounced in her shirt. His cock stiffened in his jeans at the sight.

"Cowboy, you have no idea how much I needed this outing." A long, lingering sigh left her mouth. "I don't want this to end, Emmett."

His gut tightened as she voiced the fears that mirrored his. "Maybe it won't, sweetheart."

"You don't believe that. I can hear it in your voice. I see it in your face every time you look at me. You still think there's a husband or a boyfriend looking for me, don't you?"

"It's one possibility." He hated where this discussion was headed. "We need to start back. It will be dark soon. If Cody and Bryant couldn't get past the blockage, they'll already be back at the cabin."

"They'll get past it. It hasn't rained in two days, so the conditions have surely improved. You made your case to them, and they are hell bent on finding more about my past. They might've found my car by now. Besides, they said they were going to make it to town no matter what. They want to talk to the sheriff." She rolled over to her side and faced him. "The person they find won't be me, Emmett. Married or not, I'm not her."

He cupped her chin. "You are. You just don't remember, Amber. But you will. You'll see."

"I want to be here. I want Cody and Bryant. I want you. I want to have what your parents had. Whatever I left behind could take that away from all of us. Can't you see that?"

He stood up, knowing if he remained next to her on the blanket, his willpower would crumble. "Yes, I do."

He gazed down at the beauty that was undoing all he'd built. His life was a house of cards, ready to fall to the floor, but it was all he knew. His parents were dead. His brothers had suffered so much. Amber was suffering. He would not add to everyone's pain even if it meant he had to suffer alone. God, he wanted to touch her, to take her, to kiss her, and yes, to fuck her. But he couldn't, God help him. "What do you want me to do? You might be another's woman. I have a code I live by, Amber. You might not understand that, but it means something to me. We've told you about Phase Four. We've told you about our playroom and the kind of sex we practice, right?"

She nodded, looking even more tempting than ever before.

"It's so much more than sex for me. Our lifestyle isn't for everyone, but it probably saved the twins' life and mine. Their grief was crushing after our parents died. The state came in and tried to take them away from me. I was only eighteen at the time. They were fifteen. My parents were sending me off to college. They wanted me to pursue bigger dreams than ranching."

"But you love ranching." Her words came out like breathy puffs.

"I do love ranching, but I wanted to learn about the world, about business, about everything. My mother encouraged me the most in that regard. She always said that ranching was in my blood but I needed to go out and find myself first. Once done, she believed I would return. But I never got to go. Once they died, I had one focus, one goal—keeping my brothers together with me."

"So you never went to college."

"I got my degree online just last year. Business."

"It's not the same though, is it?"

How could she read him so easily?

"No. But that's what I'm trying to tell you, sweetheart. Life sucks sometimes. We have to do things we don't want to sometimes. My brothers mattered more to me than college, than traveling the world. Did I have some resentment? Of course, I'm human. But then Mr. Gold took us under his wing. I was the youngest Dom at the club.

Once Cody and Bryant came of age, they, too, followed me into the life. It centered all of us. Now, it is part of our DNA."

"Are you afraid I won't fit into your world, Emmett? Cody has told me about BDSM in length. It's clearly about the bond of trust between submissive and Dom. I trust you. I trust Cody and Bryant. Truthfully, I am more than a little curious about your locked-up playroom. I want to have my own discovery about the lifestyle. Does that make a difference to you?'

Fuck, it did. More than a little. In fact, his cock and balls were standing up and cheering. He gazed down at this woman who inhabited his every waking thought and every nightly dream. How easy it would be to strip her of her clothes and take her on an introduction into BDSM. He closed his eyes and tried to steady himself. The whiskey in his veins was softening his resolve.

Once Cody and Bryant returned, the truth would be known and this dream would be over. Amber would go back to the life she'd forgotten and he and his brothers would go on without her. But how could he let that happen? He couldn't imagine a single day without seeing her, without talking to her, without touching her.

"Let's table this discussion for later, Amber. We need to head back."

"God, you are so infuriating." She stood up and pointed her tiny index finger into the center of his chest. "I didn't take you for a coward, but that is exactly what you are, Emmett Stone. A coward."

"Be careful, missy. Be very careful." She was pushing it.

"Chicken. Fraidycat. Quitter. Weakling. Call yourself whatever you want, cowboy. I see you for who you are—hiding behind your made-up ethics to keep from taking a real chance on a real woman who is standing right in front of you, ready to give herself fully to you."

He'd learned Amber could be a brat, sassy, and full of fire, but that was just part of her allure. How she was acting now was over the line—way over. She was trying to push his buttons, and she was succeeding.

He grabbed both her wrists, holding her in place. “Enough. Understand?”

She spat out her words like machine gun fire. “You’re not my Dom, mister. You don’t want to be my Dom. You don’t want to be my lover. You have no hold on me, cowboy.”

More than anything, he wanted to bend her over his knee and paddle her sweet, round ass until her common sense returned. But he didn’t, knowing slapping her bare bottom until it was hot and pink with his handprints would crumble his resolve. Once begun, he would not be able to stop until his dick was inside her tight pussy. *I have to do the right thing. I must.*

Filling up his lungs to the max, he used his most commanding tone. “No. More. Talking. Missy. Do. You. Understand?”

Her eyes widened and her jaw dropped. She didn’t answer with words but did nod.

His cock was aching and his balls were heavy. He lifted her up in his arms and then placed her on Bullet’s back. He gathered up their picnic items—basket, leftovers, blanket—and handed them to Amber. “Hold these.”

“Okay,” she squeaked sweetly, better than any woman he’d ever been with.

His pulse was hard and hot in his veins. He wanted her, wanted all of her. *I have to do the right thing. She deserves at least that.*

He tugged on Bullet’s reins. “Come on, boy.”

“You’re not riding up here like we did to get to our picnic?” she asked timidly.

“No. I’m on foot.” He couldn’t risk being behind her in the saddle, holding her against his body. He just might be able to contain his hunger on the ground, but no way could he keep it at bay if he could inhale her sweet scent and touch her soft skin.

He was only human.

# Chapter Ten

Emmett sat in the chair of his parents' bedroom, mesmerized by Amber's chest rising and falling with every deep inhalation and exhalation from her lips. She'd crawled into bed and conked out right after they'd gotten back to the cabin. Five hours later, she was still asleep, and he was still watching her.

His mind wouldn't settle back enough for him to catch any zees.

The twins had to be in town by now. They might even know the full truth about who Amber really was. He didn't envy them for that knowledge. The rainstorm had made it possible for them to stay clear of Amber's real past. A week of heaven with her had created a dream that somehow there was a chance she could be his, be all of theirs. It wasn't true or possible. He knew it. Fantasies faded away. Time wouldn't heal the wound to come after she was gone. Nothing would heal that kind of heartbreak.

She was everything he'd ever dreamed of—a woman of strength and courage, a woman not afraid to challenge or to surrender, a woman of kindness and passion, and a woman so beautiful, inside and out, who could fill every day with wonder and joy for the rest of his life. Amber was that woman in every way.

He'd never believed what his parents had had together was possible for him. Now, he knew it was.

He was falling in love with Amber. He had been since he'd picked her up off the ground that first day.

Amber screamed. "No. God, no."

He leapt from the chair and pulled her into his arms. She was having a nightmare. Her eyes remained closed and she began muttering those words he'd heard the day he'd found her. "Right. Bliss. Bliss. No. Stop."

"Wake up, Amber. It's only a dream." He shook her slightly.

Her eyes fluttered open and he saw the river of tears flowing down her cheeks. "What's going on?"

"You were having a nightmare. You screamed."

"I don't remember," she cried. "Why can't I remember anything?"

He rocked her in his arms, hating the pain she was feeling. "I'm here, sweetheart. It's okay."

"No. It's not. The only thing I remember is the boy. His face. Nothing more. I know this is over." Her body shook from violent sobbing.

"Amber, you have to believe." He held her close, hoping to take away her torment.

"You don't believe in us. Whatever chance we might've had is over. I can't do this any longer. I have to face facts. You and me never had a chance. Cody and Bryant are over. I'm lost, Emmett. So very lost."

"Baby, I'm here." Her suffering was ripping her apart and killing him. He stroked her hair and rocked her trembling body.

"It's too much. I can't bear this anymore. Forgive me, but I want you. I want you, Emmett. I need you. Don't hate me for it, please."

He cradled her chin in his hand. "Look at me, Amber."

She blinked and more tears fell down her gorgeous face.

"I can never hate you. You want to know the truth? I want you. I want you forever, God help me. If some man comes through that door to claim you as his own, I'm not sure I would be able to let you go."

"Oh, Emmett." Her voice cracked and the cutest smile he'd ever seen spread out over her face, enhancing her already-too-beautiful looks.

Her sweet mouth continued to quiver, tempting him beyond reason, beyond his capacity to resist. Licking his own lips, he placed the tip of his finger on her lush lips. "Shh, baby. Fuck, I've tried to hold myself back, deny myself what I've craved. I should wait. You and I both know I should, but I can't. Not any longer." He cupped her breasts through her shirt. "Right or wrong, I've wanted to touch you here." He used his thumbs to tease both her nipples.

She closed her eyes and whimpered her approval.

He cast aside his decency for something more demanding, a deep, unrelenting need. He needed to kiss her, to feel her mouth surrender to his, to enjoy her whimpers of ecstasy in his ears.

He leaned in to capture her mouth with his, feeling the very last ounce of his willpower evaporate inside him. As their lips pressed together, his hunger exploded inside him. Her soft lips tasted sweet, like warm honey. He stroked her bottom lip with his tongue until she parted her mouth ever so slightly—an invitation for a deeper kiss. Her breaths came faster and faster into his mouth as he massaged her breasts. He sank into her, tasting utter rapture. Having her in his arms might be a misstep, but the only thing he could feel was so overwhelming, so staggering, he had to sample more of Amber, much more.

* * * *

Amber couldn't get her bearings.

Emmett's kiss was melting her into a puddle. This cowboy sure knew how to undo a woman. He cradled her hips in his broad hands, and her temperature shot up several degrees.

Her mind whirled like a top. Being in his arms had been what she wanted. Wasn't it? She broke free of his kiss.

His hot gaze made her tremble. "You knock my socks off, sweetheart."

God, how good his words sounded to her.

She'd been asleep and awoke in his arms. According to him, she'd been having a nightmare, though she couldn't remember a thing about it except the face of the sweet boy.

Emmett leaned back into her, kissing her eyes closed.

How she'd dreamed of this moment, of him making love to her until dawn. He'd been a true gentleman, the most logical of all of them, the one who insisted they all do the suitable thing and keep their desires under control—until now. She knew they would regret it later, but she couldn't stop him. She opened her eyes and gazed into his. "I'm okay now. Whatever I was dreaming is gone. You don't have to try to comfort me."

"Is that so?" His eyelids narrowed, making him look sexier and more dangerous. "I'm in control here, baby, not you. Time for you to learn what it really means to submit to a Dom."

He pinched her ass with his thick fingers, inflicting a burning sting that quickly modulated into a tremble that reached all the way into her pussy.

She gulped a mouthful of air into her lungs. His words made her feel fragile and tiny. God, he was so big and muscular. What would it feel like to be truly dominated by him? His brothers had given her a little taste of what it meant to be subdued, and she'd loved every second of their commanding lovemaking. But now, with Emmett, she realized that had only been a little peek into the lifestyle they practiced. Where Cody and Bryant had been forceful, Emmett was clearly ready to conquer her completely. Deep down, that had been what she'd wanted all along. She reached up and felt his steely biceps built up from years of working this ranch. What woman wouldn't want to be held by such a man? Emmett made her feel safe, and right now, he was making her feel really warm.

He lifted her up into his arms. "Time to introduce you to the playroom."

Oh God. She'd looked at its locked door, always wondering what kind of pleasure treasures it hid. "Emmett, are you sure?"

He kissed her again, silencing her. His tongue shot past her lips into her hungry mouth. "What color are you?" His deepest tones vibrated along her skin. Such force both terrified and thrilled her.

"Green, Sir."

"That's my girl."

He smiled, rendering her body into a pliable bundle, soft as down. Every part of her wanted to obey his commands, every one. She wanted to please him. Her surrender would be total and complete. Tonight was theirs. Whatever news came back with the twins she could face with Emmett by her side. He was pure strength. He was safety. He was her cowboy, if not for forever, for tonight.

As he carried her into the hallway, Amber closed her eyes and leaned into his chest. She heard him open a drawer and heard a set of keys jingle. He was really taking her to the playroom.

Before going to bed with Bryant and Cody, the latter cowboy had sat with her several nights on the porch telling her the ins and outs of BDSM. She'd been aware Cody was informing her of the sexual play he and his brothers practiced as another way to tempt her. The more she'd learned, the more her curiosity had grown. Now, Emmett was going to show her the ropes. Was she really ready for it?

She opened her eyes as he unlocked the door, continuing to hold her with only one arm. God, the man was strong. He kicked it open with his boot. The room was pitch-black. A shiver shot up and down her spine.

Emmett flipped on a switch, and the room's contents came into view, lit by the soft glow of rope lights surrounding the ceiling's edge. "Welcome to the playroom, love."

She glanced around the space, taking it all in. The square room was bigger than she'd imagined, at least twenty feet in both directions. The walls were painted black and there were no windows, which she'd actually expected. The far wall, opposite the doorway they were standing in, was lined with shelves from floor to ceiling. On them was every kind of sex toy imaginable—dildos, vibrators, clamps, paddles, plugs, and many more she couldn't identify. On the wall to their left was a large wooden cabinet and a metal cage.

A cage? Her heart pounded in her chest so hard she thought she might pass out.

"Should I put you in the box tonight?" Emmett's tone worked her into a state of shivers.

"No, Sir. Please."

He laughed with a playful wickedness that caused her to hold her breath. "Maybe I will and maybe I won't. Keep looking at my room, baby."

She obeyed instantly. The wall to the right had four metal rings, two up high and two next to the floor.

"We use those to restrain submissives like you, Amber."

*Like me?* She could feel the truth of his proclamation about her into her very flesh. Surrendering to a man, a real man, a Dom, was her nature. Had it always been so, even in her past? Her gut clenched at the thought.

"You've drifted off, haven't you?"

She nodded, ashamed of herself. She wanted to please him, to make him proud. This was their time, and she didn't want to waste a second of it.

"See that?" He pointed to the odd-looking bench in the center of the room. It reminded her of a massage table somewhat, even though it was lower and smaller. Instead of flat, it was bent in the middle, creating a kind of peak. Had she gotten massages in her past?

"Gone again, aren't you, sub?" His tone held a sharp edge that cut into her.

"Yes, Sir. I'm sorry."

"Time to get you out of that busy head of yours, sweetheart. The spanking bench will be perfect for me to get you focused. What color are you?"

*Spanking bench?* "Green, Sir." Did he mean to spank her? Her clit tingled at the thought.

"But first, I want you out of your clothes." He lowered her to the floor until she was standing on her own two feet. He took a single step back from her. He trailed his big, beautiful eyes up and down her body, causing butterflies to take flight in her belly. "Strip for me, pet."

Her pulse quickened. He clearly wanted a show from her. Though she wasn't confident in her ability to give him one, Amber would try the best she could.

She unbuttoned the top buttons of her shirt. No bra. God, would she ever be able to wear one again? Her hands began to tremble, and she couldn't seem to get the third button unfastened.

Emmett reached forward and placed his hands on hers. "You're doing great, Amber."

Happy tingles spread through her as her cowboy Dom assisted her with the buttons. When he parted the shirt and exposed her breasts, she watched his pupils actually dilate.

"My God, these are the most gorgeous tits I've ever laid my eyes on." She reveled in his praise as he cupped her mounds tenderly. "Amber, understand that I will never tire of playing with these. Ever."

"Yes, Sir." She loved the feel of his fingertips on her flesh. As he began kneading her breasts deliciously, her breathing came faster and faster, her need for more air growing with each of his caresses.

"Even though you look so sexy in a man's shirt, it's time to see you with it off." He removed the plaid shirt easily and tossed it to the ground, leaving her in only the boxer shorts. "Keep your hands at your sides, sweetheart, until I say you can move them."

She nodded, showing him her compliance to his command.

Her whole wardrobe had consisted of clothes from the brothers' teenager pasts. Western shirts, like the one on the floor now, or T-shirts were her only tops. Boxers or much-too-big jeans were the only clothing for her lower half. She preferred the boxers to the jeans. The latter required her to constantly pull them up to keep from exposing her ass. Besides, with the shirts or tees being so long, she never worried walking around the cabin in the boxers. But she wasn't walking anywhere right now. She was under the spell of a cowboy Dom, and with only the white boxers on, felt a hot flash rip through her body at being so exposed to him. Suddenly, she felt nervous again.

Amber wrapped her arms around her chest even though she knew it was foolish. Emmett had just been touching them.

"Bad girl. Already disobeying me?"

She looked down at her feet, unable to look him in the eye. A hot shiver shook her entire body. She felt him cradle her chin and tenderly push up.

She looked directly into his big, sexy eyes and felt her legs turn to noodles. His arms came around her, keeping her from falling. God, how the man could read her inside and out.

"Baby, you're okay. We're okay. Trust me. What color are you?"

She closed her eyes and gave it some thought. Anxiety ripped through her like a storm but so did desire, and its winds were stronger than her worry. "Green, Sir. I'm green."

He smiled broadly. "What was it like to be with my brothers, Amber?"

Her cheeks got so hot she wondered if they would melt off her face. "I'm not sure what you mean."

His hands shot to her nipples and he delivered a sweet pinch, making her ache deep down. Then she felt the moistness between her legs.

"How was it being with two men at the same time?" His lurid question made her face burn even hotter.

"It was good," she said, noticing how soft and breathy her words were. Not surprising, since getting enough air was becoming more and more difficult.

The pinch came again and more wetness with it. "Talk plainly to me, love. You know about our family, about our desire to have one woman to share. You say you're in love with them. Make me believe you. I want to hear what worked for you, what made you crazy for more, what got you hot. Did they pinch your tits, too?"

She nodded. Had she ever talked dirty before? She wasn't sure since her past was caged behind the wall in her mind.

"What else, Amber?"

"They touched my sex," she blurted out and felt a tremble roll through her.

Emmett stroked her hair. "You can do better than that, baby. Use explicit words for me. Understand?"

"Yes, Sir."

"Go on. What did Cody and Bryant do that pleased you?"

"They were amazing. So strong and so very sexy. They have hearts of gold, Emmett."

"Sex, love. Tell me about the sex. It will turn us both on hearing wicked words come out of that pretty little mouth of yours. Spill the details. Now."

Was his insistence that she tell him everything about yesterday Emmett's way of making sure she would be able to settle into being shared by the three of them? They must have been looking their whole lives for a woman they could love together.

"First, Bryant kissed me. God, what a kiss it was. It went through my whole body like a warm blast. He touched me so tenderly."

"Where did he touch you?" Emmett's tone was quite deep and filled with delicious hunger. His eyes narrowed, making him look like a predator about to pounce.

"Everywhere, Sir."

"Show me."

She moved her hands up to her neck, recalling how wonderful it had been to have her cowboy's fingers on her. "My neck. He even stroked my hair. Then he touched my arms, causing me to shiver." She moved her fingers down her body as Bryant had done. "He stroked my breasts wonderfully. Then he kissed his way down my belly." Her heart was pounding in her chest.

Emmett nodded his approval. "And?"

"He went down on me, Sir. He licked my…pussy."

"You're doing great. Keep talking, sub." He removed his shirt, and her eyes took in his muscled frame. His abdomen was a shredded piece of art.

"His mouth felt like a miracle on me. I came."

He walked over to the cabinet and put on a leather vest. It only made him look even sexier, which was hard to believe. But there he was, standing a couple of feet from her, looking like a god, a champion, a man who could make a woman scream from total release.

"Was that when Cody found you two in bed?"

She nodded. "He wasn't jealous. Not one bit. He jumped in bed and…well, you know. You saw us."

"You were doing so good, pet. Don't blow it now. Tell me what happened next. I want to hear how it made you feel. Don't leave anything out, understand?"

"Yes, Sir." Pleasing him, making him proud, was the only thing she wanted to do now. "I loved the feeling of being claimed by them."

"My turn to claim you," he whispered fiercely.

She knew for sure that Emmett wanted her, just like Cody and Bryant had told her. Even he'd admitted some to that, though she hadn't ever been certain he was telling the truth or just trying to pacify her. But Emmett bringing her to his and his brothers' playroom, dressing in his sexy leather vest, teaching her about his sexual practices in BDSM, asking her to tell him every intimate, naughty detail about her lovemaking with his brothers was so much evidence—proof positive—he was interested in her.

"Look at me, sub. Take all of me in."

"Yes, Sir." She gazed at the cowboy standing right in front of her.

Emmett had rescued her. He'd been kind and a gentleman. When she'd asked him to look away so that she could bathe, he'd done it so politely. But there wasn't an ounce of politeness in Emmett now. She wasn't about to ask him to look away, though he looked so daunting to her right now. He was a Dom to be taken seriously, to be obeyed always, and to be overwhelmed by tonight.

"Tell me what you see, sub," he commanded.

"I see you, Sir. You are powerful and manly. You are dangerous and decent. You're direct and fair. You care deeply and are stubborn, too."

"That I am, sweetheart. That I am." His lusty eyes were making every hair on her arms stand on end. He stroked her hair gently. "Amber, you are just what I need. My whole life I've been lost until you. Time for me to prove to you that I'm what you need, love."

Her trembles threatened to knock her to the ground, but somehow she was able to remain on her feet.

He pinched her nipples, and her entire body tingled with applause. Her breaths came faster and faster as he licked her taut tips with his tongue. When he tugged on her hair as he sucked on her breasts, her pussy got even wetter.

"I'm going to awaken your body, Amber, in ways you never knew possible," he whispered between licks. "I know just what you need."

"What do I need, Sir?" she asked. "Are you sure you know?"

His hand came to the top of the boxers' elastic. He curled his fingers around it. She gasped as he slipped the underwear to her ankles.

"You've been bad, Amber—a very bad sub."

Her jaw dropped. "Sir?"

A wicked grin spread across his face. He cradled her chin in his big, manly hand and then she felt his other hand cover her pussy. "Nice and wet, just like I knew you would be. Thank you, pet. I'm going to enjoy tasting your cream and feeling your soaked pussy around my dick. But before that, I must decide what to do about your disobedience."

Her heart jumped up in her throat. "What did I do wrong, Sir?"

He laughed. "Nothing too bad, love. When you questioned whether I knew what you needed or not, you earned yourself a nice spanking. Never doubt my ability to know what you need. I always will know."

"I'm really sorry, but I was nervous."

He kissed her forehead. “I know. You’re doing quite well for your first time in the playroom, Amber. Your infraction wasn’t egregious, but it does give me an opportunity to teach. Plus, it’s so clear to me that your sexual nature is submissive. Do you want to please me? Do you want to learn more about my brothers’ and my lifestyle?”

“Oh, yes!” Excitement spread through her like wildfire. “I want that more than anything. I will do anything you ask, Sir. You’ll see.”

“I want you to be totally honest with me, pet. ‘Anything’ is a serious word. You have boundaries. Everyone does. We might even discover one tonight, but I doubt it. The job of a Dom is to push a sub to explore her limits, to open her mind and body for more pleasure. Sweet anxiety isn’t a bad thing, love, but utter terror is quite another. What state are you in?”

“Green, Sir.”

“You don’t have to wait for me to ask, Amber, to tell me your state using the colors. You don’t need my permission for that. I will ask from time to time. I’m reading your body language, your breathing, your tone as best I can. I’m quite good at it, but this is our first time together. I have a job, but so do you. Understand?”

She did. “Yes. I understand, Sir.” Then, to prove it to him, she added. “I’m green, Sir. Totally green.”

“Good girl. Keep your pretty little feet in these boxers. I want you to imagine it’s impossible to move out of them. If you dare to, you will disappointment me and your ass will burn even more. Understand?”

She looked down at the fabric and shivered. “Yes, Sir.”

He laughed and kissed her on the lips, causing her toes to curl. “You can use other words, pet. I want you to describe what you’re feeling. Tell me what is going through your pretty head about these boxers. You can’t run. Hell, you can’t even take a step with them around your ankles this way, can you?”

“No, Sir.” Her nipples ached and her clitoris tingled from his low-toned words.

"Be clear. Tell me what it feels like to be constrained this way."

She closed her eyes and concentrated on what emotions she sensed inside her. "A little anxious."

"Keep your eyes closed for me." Emmett moved behind her. He was tracing his fingers over her skin, from her neck and down her back. It was having a heady impact on her. "Tell me more. Why do you feel that way, do you think?"

She gulped as his hands took hold of her ass and began to squeeze. "Green," she blurted.

"I know. We're in sync. Can you feel it?"

She could. "Yes. I can, Sir."

The realization of their harmony, creating their own special music, thrilled her. His touch was like a maestro's baton, awakening a concert of sensations with each passing refrain. She was his strings, his woodwinds, his brass, and his percussion.

"The boxers at your ankles, pet? More." His command got her mind back in focus.

"I love them there, Sir, though it does make me jumpy a little."

"Is 'jumpy' a bad thing?"

She thought about that for a moment. "No. I like being a little unbalanced with you."

"Fuck, you say all the right things, Amber. It's going to be tough to keep my head around you. That's for certain."

"What did I say, Sir?" She wasn't sure but definitely wanted to know.

"Two words, love—'with you.' Trust is something every Dom works to achieve, and here you are, the most beautiful woman in the world, telling me you trust *me*." He reached around her and cupped her breasts. "I had no idea how wonderful it would be to fall for you, Amber."

She leaned her head back into his chest. "We're here, now, cowboy…I mean, Sir. I'm completely elated."

"I still have to spank you, though. I haven't forgotten that."

She hadn't either. A robust, animated tremble moved across her skin, landing between her legs like a crashing timpani.

Suddenly, he lifted her up in his arms, and new sensations marched inside her body. Knowing he was going to spank her called to a deep, secret longing inside her, and yet her nerves were stretched out and taut. What would it feel like to be spanked by him? To have her ass's flesh stinging from his paddling? Her heart raced fast in her chest, and her mouth dried up. She licked her lips as he lowered her facedown onto the bench she'd seen when entering the room.

"This is a spanking horse, pet. I'm going to leave the boxers at your ankles. For tonight, they will be the only restraint on your legs. Your wrists are another story."

She wondered what he had in mind for a split second. When he clamped two pairs of handcuffs, one for each arm, to the bench, she knew.

"Too tight or just right?" he asked.

"Green, Sir. I'm green."

He patted her bottom gently with his open hand, and she felt more moisture slip from her pussy. Had she ever been so wet in her life? She couldn't remember, of course, but doubted it.

"I'm going to put a plug in your pretty ass, pet, the way Cody did." How did Emmett know that? The three must've talked about what had happened.

She gasped. "Yes Sir." It had been an intense sensation. She longed to feel it again.

He chuckled. "I'm getting your ass ready to take a cock. And I'm going to take your pussy as well. They are both mine. Mine, Cody's, and Bryant's. Understand?"

She nodded.

"Trust me, sweetheart."

She wanted to make him proud. "Yes, Sir. I'll do my best."

He stepped to the table that was filled with every sex device imaginable. "This is a little bigger than the one Cody used, love."

Still held to the bench by the handcuffs, she moved her head to look his direction. In one hand he held a bottle of lubricant and in the other was the fearsome toy he was planning on putting in her ass.

She gasped, feeling her heart skip several beats. "It's so big, Sir."

"I know what I'm doing, sub." His words were firm and shook her from head to toe.

Had she screwed up already? He'd brought her to this most intimate space in the cabin, the room she'd been more than a little curious about, and what did she do? Push at him. Tears welled up in her eyes. "I know. I'm sorry."

He knelt down so that their faces were only a couple of inches apart. "Do you trust me, pet?"

The more he called her "pet," "love," "sweetheart," the more she did trust him, and the more she wanted to please him. "Yes, Sir."

"What state are you in?"

"Green," she said, though it might have been the palest green ever.

"That's my girl."

She watched as he lubed his fingers.

"Deep breath, pet."

She obeyed instantly.

"Blow it out in one big breath for me."

Again, she heeded his command. As the last of the air left her mouth, she felt one of his fingers pierce her anus. She whimpered at the stinging intrusion.

"Breathe for me."

Gasping for oxygen, she stuttered, "Y–Yes, S–Sir."

He added another finger and stretched her ass more, readying it for the intimidating plug. "I like seeing you this way, pet. So beautifully submissive." His last words came out quite dominant, and yet she could hear a kindness in them as well.

His one hand continued to spread her anus wider, causing the sting to ripen into mouthwatering thirst. He'd turned her into a colossal bundle of yearning, of desire, of need.

"Open your legs for me, pet."

In a flash, she responded.

"Great. One more big breath for me, sweetheart."

She filled her lungs all the way until her breasts were pressing even harder against the bench's leather.

"Excellent. Blow it out like before."

She did and felt him push the plug into her ass. A quick bout of pain rolled through her. The thing was massive. She bit her lip as he shoved it in all the way. After the widest part of the toy moved past her tight spot, the thing was locked inside her, her anus clamping down on it like a vise.

"This will stay inside you, pet, the whole time I'm spanking your ass."

"Yes, Sir." Her words seemed to be softer and more breathy than normal. No surprise, since her pulse was hot and fast, making her head swim and her breathing labored.

"Time for your punishment, sweet sub." The raw emotion in his voice wasn't lost on her. His Dom side sat in the front seat now, and instead of making her cringe in fear, she shifted her hips so that her ass rose to some degree. She was ready. More than ready. She wanted to know what it felt like to have a man dominate her in this way. Not just any man. Emmett. Emmett Stone. Her cowboy. Her rescuer. Her Dom. The man she wanted to spend the rest of her life with.

The first slap of Emmett's hand on her ass jerked a squeak from her lips. The burn to her backside was something that ignited a mix of embarrassment and lust. As his slaps continued on, her pussy clenched and her clit throbbed. The plug inside her added to the intensity, just as he'd promised. She tried to remain still on the bench but couldn't. Instinct was taking over, and she shifted from side to side in failed attempts to avoid his big hand.

Again and again, he spanked her backside, which was burning like a bonfire. Heat reached deep into her body, igniting a flood of desire and a sea of new sensations.

Suddenly, the spanking stopped. Just as quickly, she missed the sweet punishment. "Green, Sir," she said, hoping he would continue. She wasn't ready for his amazing discipline to end. Not yet anyway. Her body was only just now settling into a slow, delicious burn from his slaps. She didn't want that to stop.

She felt Emmett's hand cup her bottom, and her pussy dampened even more.

"I love how you are responding to this, pet." His words were deep and deliberate, making her tremble. "You know you deserve this for disobeying me earlier, don't you?"

"Yes, Sir. I can take more, Sir. Green, Sir. I was bad." She turned to him and saw the frown on his face and knew she'd overstepped. She gulped as she gazed at Emmett, full-on Dom.

"Don't be bratty, sub. I'm in charge in here. Always. Don't try to get the upper hand in here. I know what I'm doing. I've been doing this for a very long time." His hand came down on her ass a little harder than previously. The burn it delivered was a few degrees hotter, too. "This pretty pink ass is ready for a paddle. Color?" His last word reminded her of another kind of slap. He clearly wouldn't tolerate disobedience.

"I'm green, Sir," she said, but in the back of her mind a spot of yellow appeared. How far could she go with him, with this kind of sex? The heat between her thighs told her she could go a little farther. How far? She wasn't sure but was willing to find out.

Emmett walked back to the table of toys. "Rules, Amber. Protocols. That's part of BDSM, but only a part. It's important. It helps all of us—Doms and subs—have a path to follow. Enforcing rules is a two-way street, love. You saying 'red' lets me know I've crossed a line. I give you instructions and you understand what I expect. Sound simple? It isn't. It takes practice, a lot of practice. The more we play, the more we will understand each other. I'm in your head now, but after a few months, I will be able to anticipate anything that comes into that pretty head of yours."

Four of his words transformed her into a buzzing heap of excitement—"after a few months." Her heart leapt for joy and her body sizzled with longing. She needed him to take her, to fill her, to claim her.

"Rules sound good to me, Sir."

He froze in his tracks.

"What's wrong, Sir?"

"Nothing, sub. Don't worry about a thing. I'm in charge, remember?" Something about his tone did trouble her, but she couldn't put her finger on it. Had she said something wrong? She wasn't sure.

"Yes, Sir. You're in charge."

He nodded his approval and began rifling through his assortment of toys once again. She let out a silent sigh. Why did doubt come so easily to her? Emmett was still on board in every way. Trust was her job, her only job.

When she saw him pick up a scary-looking black paddle, trust seemed to scamper away inside her for a moment. Gazing at the dark shade of the monstrous thing caused another color to vibrate at the back of her throat. Red—the one word that would hit the brakes completely. Her lips vibrated silently, chewing on the single syllable.

Emmett stared at her with his big knowing eyes. "What color are you, Amber?"

Why was she afraid of the paddle? Sure, certainly a woman ticd to a bench with a powerful man about to use the thing on her backside would be alarmed. But she wasn't just any woman. She was Emmett's woman. He wasn't just any man. He was her Dom.

"Yellow," she confessed, hoping he wouldn't be ashamed of her.

"Good girl. Very good." He put the paddle back where he'd gotten it. "I wanted to test you and you did amazing. Excellent, love. Really good work."

"I don't understand. If you want to use that thing on me, I think

I—"

Another slap from his manly hand landed in the middle of her ass, conveying another sweet sting. Who knew a spanking could be so erotic? She certainly had thought it might, but it surpassed even her expectations. Her pussy was drenched and her clit throbbed to be caressed.

"Who is in charge in here, sub?"

"You are, Sir," she said, resisting the urge to ground her mound into the bench for much-needed relief, believing he wouldn't care for her to do that.

He patted her ass lightly. "Do you trust me?"

"I do. I trust you."

"I can see you do, love. You wanted a lesson in BDSM. I wanted you to experience pain and vulnerability. You're responding just as I knew you would. Isn't this exciting to you?"

"God, yes. Yes, Sir. I–I don't know enough words to tell you how much."

He pushed her hair aside, and their eyes met. "I hear your words and I hear your body. Amber, I can sense more than you can ever say."

Leaning into her, he kissed her eyes closed. She felt his lips on her nose, then her cheeks. Then he claimed her mouth with his own. His kiss overwhelmed her with its intensity, its possessiveness. Tingles jetted through her body.

Emmett removed the handcuffs and guided her to turn on the bench until she was facing up, *facing him*. Another kiss began. His probing tongue made her wonderfully dizzy, his mouth heating her up from the inside out. He crushed her against his chest with his hand on her back, his lips pressing against her like a triumphant victor. The friction of their bodies made her nipples peak and throb even more.

He ended their kiss and gazed at her with his piercing eyes. "You're something else, sweetheart. You'll be the ruin of me for sure." His tone was quite serious, evoking a fresh wave of shivers in her.

He leaned in and kissed her again, and her toes curled tightly. His tongue moved along the seam of her lips. His hands slid down to the curve of her waist, and she wrapped hers around his neck. Being dominated by Emmett filled her with excitement and desire. Right now, in this space, on this bench, she didn't give a damn about anything else. The wall that held her memories locked away, her worries, her insecurities, all of it fell away as her cowboy melted her into a puddle with kisses and caresses.

He released her lips, now swollen and throbbing from their overwhelming kiss. "Sweetheart, tell me what you want."

The past week rolled up into this single moment of authenticity she could no longer hold back. She'd told him in so many words previously, but now the truth shot out of her like a rocket. "I want you, Emmett Stone. I love you and I want you."

His eyes burned with lust and passion, and her temperature rose. "You're so tiny and feminine, baby. Perfect. That's what you are." His voice sounded more like it came from a hungry beast than a man. "Tonight is about you and your pleasure." The quiet calm of his voice reminded her once again of how vulnerable and exposed she felt.

"Green, Sir."

"Leave everything to me." He licked the tip of her left breast's nipple, and a hot tremble shot deep into her pussy.

The more he suckled on her breasts, the more sparks fired inside her. A fathomless want mushroomed in her pussy. Needing relief, she moved her fingers to her throbbing clit, which was drenched from her passionate drops.

"No, pet." He grabbed her wrists and pulled her hands up until her fingertips were touching his thick, manly lips. "I will take care of you. You don't have to do a thing but feel and enjoy. Understand?"

"Yes, Sir."

He nodded and parted his lips, pulling her fingertips into his mouth. The masculine moan that emitted from his throat vibrated along her skin. She felt like her body was floating to the ceiling.

Once again, he swallowed her nipple. When his teeth tightened on it lightly, the throbbing in her fleshy tip caused her back to arch up from the bench.

She was drowning in hot waves, and she bit her lip, trying but failing to stay above the lusty surface.

Emmett's head came up from his meal of her breasts. "You're too much, baby. Fuck, from head to toe, you're flat-out flawless." His words were filled with smoldering devotion and fiery eagerness.

"You, too, cowboy. You're perfect."

"I can't wait to taste you." His fingers lightly touched her breasts. Then he slowly trailed them down her stomach to her clit, grazing her there. More need than she thought possible exploded inside her.

His fingertips threaded through her pussy, raising her temperature even more. "You like that, don't you, sweetheart?"

She placed her hands on his muscled shoulders. "Yes, Sir. Very much." A bright green appeared in her mind's eye. She was ready for whatever he would bring. All of it. All of him.

He continued teasing her pussy's wet folds, causing her to claw his flesh. "I'll make sure you're totally satisfied, Amber. Trust me."

He moved down the bench between her legs. His hot breath danced like a hot breeze on her aching pussy and throbbing clit.

"God, this is the most beautiful pussy I've ever seen in my life."

His words sent her to the sky, but when his tongue grazed her clit, she went beyond the moon. His licks turned her body into a live wire of shivers. Her desire grew and grew and grew until she thought she would go completely insane. When his tongue pierced her slit, a hot bolt sliced deep into her pussy, like a knife into butter.

"Give me your sweet cream, baby. I want my face drowning in your juices." Emmett lowered his head back between her thighs.

Feeling his teeth capture her clit sent overwhelming sensations through her. "God, yes!" Her toes curled, and she wrapped her legs around his head as he sent a couple of his fingers down her channel, caressing her in that special spot. She pounded the bench with her fists, her pussy clenching again and again into her cowboy's assault.

Her pussy clenched against Emmett's hot, sensual storm of fingers, lips, and tongue. When his hands grabbed her by the hips, pulling her in closer, she moaned loudly. His constant licks of her swollen clit worked her into an uncontrollable lather of wildness and release. Unable to hold back any longer, she screamed into his intimate kiss on her pussy. Filled with rapturous release, she surrendered to the sensations of her orgasm, an orgasm so consuming and overwhelming, she wondered if she might actually pass out. Again, another wave of fresh trembles, stronger than before and much hotter, shook every nerve in her body. Ablaze with white heat, she felt her pussy clench, again and again, flattening her completely out.

"O–Oh, God!" Her mind was whirling like a top. The buzzing in her body was making her deliciously dizzy and wonderfully spent. Every inch of her was releasing energy, tons of it.

Emmett had delivered intense oral pleasure that was astonishing. What would his cock inside her pussy feel like? She couldn't wait to find out.

The influx of vibes from her climax went on and on for some time. Her world was this room, currently with a population of two. She and Emmett, one of her cowboy loves.

After some time, she felt his feathery fingers on her legs. He massaged his way down to her ankles, still restrained by the boxers he'd kept on her.

Never had she imagined sex could be like this. This was more than a simple wish. Need and a craving to be filled by this man who had changed her world, who had rescued her from God knew what, swallowed her up entirely.

"P–Please, Sir. Fuck me."

"Shh." He removed the plug from her ass in a single movement. "Stop grabbing the reins, Amber. Remember, I'm in charge." Emmett moved up her body, dropping kisses on every inch of her skin. When he was back on top of her, face-to-face, he kissed her, and she felt his hot hunger. Everything inside her went topsy-turvy.

Slowly, her heartbeats and breaths backed down bit by bit. Sugar-coated fatigue soothed her edges. The outline of Emmett's fully erect cock stretched the denim of his jeans, but he didn't make a move to impale her pussy.

Instead, he lifted her up in his arms.

"That's the end of tonight's lesson, sweetheart." His words were tender but his eyes stormed with starvation.

"You're not going to fuck me?" she asked meekly.

"That's right, Amber. You're spent. You did great, really great, but it has been a very long day for you. Time to get you to bed. Time for you to sleep."

He was holding the reins. He was in charge. He'd made that very clear and she accepted that now. Still, a little tinge of worry shot through her. "Yes, Sir."

Amber leaned her head into his naked, muscled chest as he carried her out of the playroom and to the bedroom.

One thought twisted her weary brain into a tight knot as he placed her on the bed. *Is he still holding something back from me?*

# Chapter Eleven

Bryant looked around the sheriff's office. It was a no-frills, utilitarian room, which was appropriate since it was just one of three other rooms of the jailhouse without bars. The two guest chairs were nondescript and not very comfortable. The desk held only a computer, nothing else. The shelves on the wall behind it held only manuals and books, nothing personal, nothing superficial, nothing that gave a clue to the person who had won the right in the closest election in the history of the county to sit in the only luxury item here—the big leather chair behind the desk.

Bryant didn't need any clues. He knew the man who had occupied the space for the past two years quite well. Sheriff Jason Wolfe was only a few years older than him and Cody and only a couple months younger than Emmett.

Jason and his two brothers, Mitchell and Lucas, had grown up in Destiny, just like Bryant and his brothers. But the Wolfe brothers weren't tight like them. In fact, they were worlds apart in so many ways. Jason, who had more than a few run-ins with the law during his high school years, had turned his former wild-oats-sowing nights into somber, straightlaced days that had landed him the highest office in the county last election.

"Where the fuck is he? He should've been back by now." Cody was pacing like a man isolated from any human contact awaiting the long walk down a prison's hallway to the electric chair.

He couldn't blame his twin, since that was exactly how he was feeling, too. They'd come down the mountain mostly on foot, having to dismount their horses several times due to the poor condition of the roads.

They'd come to the rockslide at The Narrows and had seen a white van on its side down the cliff. They both agreed it was too risky to climb down to see if it was Amber's, but they both knew it had to be. As they'd headed down to town, Bryant had questioned himself about the decision not to scale the cliff to the vehicle below. He and Cody had been quick to let it go for another time, saying they needed different equipment to be safe. To some extent that was true, but it wasn't the real reason they'd continued the trek, leaving the downed van behind. They were both terrified of what they would find inside the van. With Amber's identity remaining a mystery, they could fool themselves into believing her past wouldn't come crashing into their lives and take her away from them. That had been the real reason they'd not descended down to the automobile.

It had taken them all day and three hours after the sun went down to get to the city limits. Instead of heading to their house in town, they'd taken the direct route here. Jason had been out on a call in Clover, one of four other towns in the county besides Destiny. The eccentric dispatcher, Shannon Day, who was well into her sixties and was known in town for her colorful wigs and known by most, though not Jason, for her love of smoking pot, had sent out word to her boss of their need to see him.

The door opened and in came Shannon wearing large sunglasses and a shoulder-length purple wig. "The sheriff just pulled up outside. He'll be right in to talk to you."

"Thanks, Shannon." Bryant's gut tightened. He wasn't ready to know if anyone had come looking for Amber. Deep down, he knew he would never be ready. Cody had to be right. Amber was their future. Her arrival at their ranch just had to be more than coincidence.

Jason walked in, wearing his sheriff garb—tan shirt and matching pants, holstered gun and badge, and on top of his close-cropped head, his wide-brimmed hat. "Hello, fellows." He took off his hat and placed it on the hook by the only window in his office. "Shannon has already told me via the radio about your guest."

"Good to know you're ahead of the game on this one." Cody leaned forward in his chair. "What can you tell us about her, Jason?"

The sheriff walked around his desk and sat down in his leather chair. "You say she looks to be in her mid-twenties, right?" He got a pen and a pad from his desk's top drawer. He held the tip a fraction of an inch from the paper and looked directly at Cody and then at Bryant.

"That's right," Bryant answered. "Long, dark hair. Amber-colored eyes."

Jason wrote in his pad. "How tall would you say she is?"

"Five three," Cody answered. "So has anyone been looking for her or not?"

"Let's see what we can find out." The sheriff set the pad beside his keyboard and typed the only facts they had about Amber. After what seemed like an eternity, but was likely less than ten minutes, Jason pointed to the screen. "This one looks like a match."

"Fuck," Cody blurted out.

Bryant agreed. It was the only word that fit this moment. Amber had a past. Someone was looking for her.

"Hold on. This is from a Chicago precinct. No picture included. That's odd." Jason continued. "You say she's been with you for one week, right?"

"Yeah." Bryant stood up. "What does it say?"

"Chill out, Stone. Let me see what's in this report. 'Missing person' is a broad term that covers a whole host of possibilities, guys. It covers runaways, people with dementia, missing hikers, crime victims, overdue travelers, and a whole slew of others. A lot of them don't fall in a bucket that law enforcement can act on, but some do." He pointed to the screen. "If this is your girl, I'll find out. I'll call the officer who uploaded this report in the morning."

"Call him now, Jason." Bryant's heart felt like it was ripping in two.

"It's a *her,* but okay, buddy. I will."

He'd convinced himself into believing Cody was right about fate bringing Amber to them. Why had he chosen to be so reckless and foolhardy? He should've followed Emmett's advice and kept his dick in his pants. But he'd waved the white flag to his carnality, his lust, and now he would suffer and so would Amber once the people in her past came for her.

The sheriff dialed the number on the screen. "Hello, this is Sheriff Wolfe from Swanson County, Colorado. I'm calling for Officer Nicole Flowers. She is?" Bryant was hanging on Jason's every word, praying that Amber wasn't the one the Chicago PD was looking for. "Maybe you can help me. I'm calling about a missing person inquiry she put out on the national database. I'm not sure if this is your girl or not, but we do have some details that line up. Yes. You don't? I understand. Yes. I will call back in the morning. Thank you very much." He put the receiver back on the phone's cradle.

"Well?" Cody snapped.

"That was Officer Jaris Black. He works with Flowers. He didn't have any answers for me, guys, but said he would e-mail me a picture of their missing woman once he got his computer turned on. You guys willing to wait?"

"Of course," Bryant answered, dread crawling up from his belly and wrapping its claws around his throat.

"Like I said, this is likely a dead end. Most missing persons stay missing, but I'll do my best to find out who your mystery girl is. Have you considered she might've been voluntarily walking away from her life and her relationships?"

He nodded, hoping against all odds that Amber had done just that. "More than you can imagine, Jason."

Cody chimed in. "Much more."

* * * *

Emmett looked around his cabin. A week earlier, its feel had been more like barracks than a home. After Amber had pulled out candles she'd found tucked away in some drawers and other decorative items she'd discovered in the back of one of the closets, the place had been transformed from a gloomy, dank cabin into a bright, airy home. Even the fragrance of the wildflowers she'd placed in a couple of vases enhanced the feel. How long had it been since he'd felt at home anywhere? He had his brothers, for sure. They were his family and had his back always, and he had theirs. Even so, he hadn't felt at home, really at home, since losing his parents. That was, until Amber's arrival. She'd changed everything. He'd been blind to what his life and his brothers' lives had become. Now, he could see for the first time in his life.

Amber placed a plate with a sandwich and some chips in front of him. "I sure hope Bryant and Cody remember to bring the groceries I put on the list."

He and Amber had been silent on discussing his brothers' absence and pending return since before the time in the playroom together. "I'm sure they will bring you everything you asked for."

She sat across from him at the table and stared into her own plate, its contents mirroring his. "I don't know about you, cowboy, but I'm in the mood for some pasta and a nice, big salad."

"Sounds delicious, but I would be happy eating your peanut butter and banana sandwiches every meal."

She grinned and shook her head. "I doubt that."

He watched her take a bite of her lunch and imagined what it would feel like to have her sweet lips on his cock. *Fuck, there I go again.* Keeping his head around her was proving to be the hardest thing he'd ever done.

"Can I ask you a question, Emmett?" Her big golden eyes threatened to push him over the edge.

"Ask away, sweetheart."

"Why did you stop short of intercourse with me in the playroom?"

Her words hit him in the gut like a sledgehammer. "I think we should talk about something else."

She jumped up with unshed tears glistening in her eyes. "This is too much to take, Emmett. Way too much."

He didn't want to hurt her more. Being a fuckup lately seemed to be the only thing he could do. "What do you mean, baby?"

"I thought you wanted me. I thought you were into me. You're not. I know that now. You only took me to your playroom to pacify me."

"That's not true, Amber."

"Then why didn't you fuck me when you had the chance?" The angry panic in her words crushed him.

"I wanted to, baby. God, how I wanted to."

"Then why didn't you?"

"Sit and listen to me."

"Okay. But please tell me the truth, Emmett. I need to know how you feel about me."

"How I feel about you?" He shouldn't tell her. Holding back was his way, his norm. It was how he'd survived so much. But he couldn't do that to her any longer. She deserved more than that from him. She deserved the truth. "I love you, Amber. I love you so much it is killing me. I wanted to fuck you more than anything I've ever wanted in my entire life. I was about to do it, too, but when I was telling you about BDSM and the rules, the protocols, I couldn't."

"I don't understand. What does your lifestyle have to do with whether or not we make love?"

"We did make love, pet. I tasted your cream, didn't I? The sweetest nectar I've ever sampled in my life. Seeing you writhing with pleasure by the orgasm I'd given you was reward enough. I couldn't give in to my lust, my desire. I'm a Dom, not just in name but in practice, too. It means something to me to stay true to my honor. I don't know if another man has a claim on you, Amber."

"Not that again." Her tiny hands curled into fists, clearly evidence of her inner frustration. "Emmett, can't you believe I'm single? How can I have been in love in my past and not know?"

"You're sounding a lot like Cody. Yes, I can see how there's a slim chance that another holds your heart, but there is a chance, sweetheart. Until we know, I can't do more than we did before."

"Oral sex? That's okay but not anything more? Is that what you're saying to me, Sir?" The last word came out more like profanity than respect.

Anger welled up in him for her flippancy to him. He thought about throwing her over his shoulder and marching into the playroom for another round of spanking, this time with one of his other paddles, though not his big gun that had scared her. Given time, he knew she would warm up to even that one.

"Well, cowboy, are you going to enlighten me or are you going to keep me in the dark?" Her words were razor sharp but her tone betrayed her inner state.

He could see how terrified she was. So was he. Her past would show up, likely when Bryant and Cody returned. Fuck, how he wanted to whisk her away up into the most remote parts of the state where no one would ever find them.

"No sex, Amber, until we hear what my brothers learned about you. I love you, Amber. I will love you from now until the end of time. I love your submissive nature but I also love your bratty side. I love how you have made this cabin into a home. I want you by my side for the rest of my life, I do."

"But…?"

"You know, darling. You know."

Her lower lip quivered violently, but only a single tear fell from her right eye. "I do know. I don't want to wait, Emmett, but I will for you. You'll see I'm right about this. I know what love is. I'm in love with you and with Cody and Bryant. There is no way in the world any other man has my heart. You'll see." He could hear the doubt in her voice.

He stood up, came around the table, and put his arms around her. "God, I hope so, love. I really do."

She tilted her head up until their eyes locked together. "Whatever news we get, cowboy, we will stay together. I am a full-grown woman. I know what I want, and that's you and your brothers. No one is taking that away from me."

God, who would've known such a tiny thing as her would have so much strength inside her? How could someone so wonderful not be attached? He recalled what had happened right before he'd given in to his own desires and taken her into the playroom. She'd been having a nightmare. Fully conscious, she couldn't remember anything about the bad dream. Perhaps there was an asshole in her past, be it a boyfriend, fiancé, or husband. If so, whoever he was better not show his face in Destiny. If the prick did, he vowed to pound the guy into a pile of dust.

# Chapter Twelve

Amber's thoughts were heavy with dread. Though she would rather stay on the mountain in the cabin for the rest of her life, she knew she couldn't. Her past was waiting for her in Destiny.

She was fine with Emmett helping her onto his horse. They'd all agreed to the plan last night around the kitchen table. He would ride in the saddle behind her. Bryant and Cody would head to town on their own horses. She looked at the three Stone brothers, each looking like they belonged in another place and time. They weren't dime-store cowboys by any means. From their hats to their boots to the guns in the belts around their waists, they were authentic through and through, and each of them, in their own way, had captured all of her heart.

The news the twins had returned to the cabin with had put her in a kind of walking coma. She could hear them, see them, respond to them, but her mind was far away, adrift by the wall that held her memories from her.

After they'd put away the groceries last night, all three of them had tucked her into bed. Few words were spoken by any of them, but her cowboys' eyes voiced much more than their lips did. They shared a crushing apprehension that she also felt inside herself.

The officer in Chicago had e-mailed a photo to the office in Destiny. Cody and Bryant had reluctantly admitted she was a dead ringer for the woman in the picture. Sheriff Wolfe had printed off a paper copy of the image for them to bring to the cabin. For hours, she'd looked from the photo to her reflection in the bathroom mirror. With each glance, her doubt vanished, as did her hope for the future she'd dreamed of since coming to her cowboys' cabin.

It wasn't the photo that took away the future she longed for. It was the details in the report it was attached to, the details that gave the facts about her past life.

None of them had called her by her now-known name, Kathy White, but they also hadn't called her Amber since they'd read the report and seen the picture. Chicago was her home, not this cabin. But of all the facts she'd read about herself, only one continued to swirl in her head again and again.

"Ready, sweetheart?" Emmett said behind her.

She nodded, too afraid to speak aloud. *I'm married.*

* * * *

Cody left his steed's back for the ground. Less than ten words had been uttered between the four of them. Without a doubt, the heavy gloom hanging over him also was hanging over Emmett, Bryant, and Amber, the woman he wanted to spend the rest of his life with. But he was no longer certain he would have such a future.

Ever since leaving Jason's office yesterday morning, his heart had been shredded into a scrap pile of loss and pain. His faith had crumbled into ashes the moment he'd gazed at the photo sent from the officer in Chicago. Either she had a twin or the woman in the picture was Amber, which meant she was married. Though he'd tried his best, he'd failed to stretch his imagination to the possibility she had her own duplicate, just like he did in Bryant.

"It's down here, Amber. There is no way you were in the van when it went over the side. You wouldn't have lived through that. I suspect it was pushed off when the rocks fell." He wanted to get closer to the van he and Bryant had passed twice, once on the way down to town and just last night on the way up to the cabin. It had to be Amber's, and he wanted to get inside it.

"I want to look, too," she said.

"All right, but stay next to us." Emmett dismounted and helped the woman of all their dreams to the ground.

Her tiny fingers pulled up the jeans she was wearing which were too big for her tiny feminine body. Damn, he and Bryant should've thought to get her some clothes while they were in town, but the news they'd learned from the report had sent them into a total tailspin.

She walked between Emmett and Bryant to the drop-off. They each held one of her arms. Like him, they would do anything to keep her safe. Whatever length he and his brothers needed to go to ensure she was protected from harm, they would do it.

She leaned over the edge slightly. "I see it. That's a long way down, guys."

Cody agreed. "I'm going to climb down and get whatever belongs to you and bring it back up."

"No way," she said. "You're coming with us to Destiny. That's what we all agreed to."

Her mettle was just one of the things he loved about her. "I don't remember me making that commitment, sweetheart. You head to town with my brothers. I'll join you shortly."

"Are you sure about this, bro?" his twin asked.

"Yes, I'm sure. I'm the best climber of the three of us and you know it. You might've been the calm one when Emmett broke his legs but I was the one who was able to climb down and get him."

Bryant nodded.

"Maybe that's true, but I would feel better if you waited until tomorrow when we all can be here to support you." She wasn't about to throw in the towel on what she thought he should do, and he couldn't help but love her more for it. "Emmett, don't you agree?"

Emmett shook his head. "I do not. Amber, you might think this isn't safe, but I trust Cody."

"So do I," Bryant added.

"But there's no cell service here." The worry in her voice couldn't be missed. "If he insists on doing this, shouldn't one of you two stay?"

"I grew up in these mountains, Amber." Cody gazed at the woman who he would never stop loving no matter her past or who was in it. He'd resigned himself to the fact that he might have to let her go, but he prayed it wouldn't come to that. "I know how to traverse them. I won't be long. This should take me no more than an hour and a half to get down and back up."

"Can't you wait until we talk with the sheriff? Once we finish up with him, you can take me to your house in town and we can all get a good night's sleep. Tomorrow we can head back up here. I won't be so worried then."

"Baby, I've got the best climbing gear made. Besides, I want to be prepared and know more about you before we make any decisions."

She turned and faced him with her long lashes fluttering like two frightened butterflies. "Why? What will that change? You saw the photo just like I did. How can you deny it's not me?"

"I'm not giving up on you, on us. I won't."

"But the report said that I'm married."

"It didn't say you were 'happily married.' There might be something in the van that will show me a way how I can keep you." He pointed to Emmett and Bryant. "How *we* can keep you. I have to believe that, Amber."

She'd clearly been stunned by what they'd learned from Jason. Now the cloud around her seemed to be lifting slightly. "So do I, Cody. I hope you're right."

"I am certain that I am right," he lied, wishing to calm her fears and his own. "There might even be divorce papers in your van."

* * * *

Emmett stared down at the damaged van below. "The cliff is unstable, Cody. Be careful."

"You've always said I was part monkey. This will be a piece of cake."

Bryant spoke in a quiet, calm tone. "I could stay like Amber suggested."

Cody shook his head. "I've climbed worse. Besides, she needs as much support as she can get."

Bryant nodded. "Doc, first. Then the sheriff."

"I want to get Amber's identification and whatever else will give us a clue to the pieces of her life that aren't in that report. That's what I want."

"No, Cody. You can't." Her voice was filled with worry for Cody's safety. "Please, listen to me. I'm not going anywhere no matter what anyone says. I need time to let everything sink in."

He watched intently as Cody stepped in front of her.

His brother grabbed both her hands and pulled them up to his chest. "Feel that. That's my heart, Amber. It's beating."

"Yes, I feel it."

"It will still be beating when you see me again. I promise. Trust me. I'll be fine. Go with my brothers to town. I'll be along in a flash and in my hands will be what we need to fix everything. You'll see and so will these two pessimists."

He admired his brother's tenacity and unbending faith in what might be.

She leaned in and kissed Cody. "Okay, but you better not be long. Promise me that."

"I promise, baby."

"How far is it to Destiny?" she asked.

"The roads get better after here," Bryant said. "Less than an hour, I'd say."

She turned to Emmett, and his heart thudded in his chest like a jackhammer. "Would you mind if I ride with Bryant the rest of the way?"

"I don't mind at all, sweetheart. I also understand why you want to."

"Thank you." She leaned in and kissed him on the cheek.

Her lips felt good on his skin. Too good. Emmett thought about telling her he'd changed his mind and that she should ride down to town all the way with him. But Bryant deserved time with her, too. This was likely their last time together. He would have to be satisfied with seeing her in front of his brother in the saddle. He'd admired how quickly she'd taken to horseback. Another month at the ranch, and he bet she would be broncobusting on her own. His jaw clenched tight as he doubted she would ever be back in their cabin.

"You know we're into sharing, sweetheart. Trust me, we're going to share you for the rest of our lives and you're going to love every minute of it," Cody suddenly blurted out.

Her face clouded with a heavy realization. She knew, as did Emmett, what was likely to happen once they came directly in contact with her past. She was claimed. There was no doubt about that any longer.

Cody was grasping at straws, but he wasn't about to try to tell his brother to toss his hopes aside. Let Cody have whatever fanciful dreams he needed to get through this nightmare. It would come crashing in on all of them soon enough.

## Chapter Thirteen

Amber walked through the door to the sheriff's office with Emmett in the lead and Bryant bringing up the rear. They'd been so careful with her, insisting that she be thoroughly examined by the town doctor. He'd given her a clean bill of health, as she knew he would. The doctor hadn't seen any evidence of brain damage. He'd told her that her memory would likely return at some point. The concern Emmett and Bryant had shown for her made facing the truth about her identity that much harder.

The man behind the desk had to be Sheriff Wolfe, but who was the guy in the chair opposite him? An officer from Chicago? She found it strange that he wasn't wearing a uniform.

"Jason." Emmett shook the sheriff's hand. Then he pointed to the chair next to the other guy, a few feet away from the stranger. "Sit, Amber."

"*Lubov moya*, it is you," the man said with what sounded to her to be a Slavic accent. The guy stood and reached for her, but Emmett and Bryant moved in front of her, blocking him from moving closer. "What the hell is this? Who are these two broken-down cowpokes, Sheriff?"

"Emmett and Bryant Stone, two of the three who rescued your wife, Mr. White."

She gasped and her knees buckled under her. She would've fallen to the floor, too, if Emmett and Bryant hadn't responded so quickly. *Wife? This is my husband.*

"They look a lot like gunslingers to me." The man's squinty eyes fixed on Emmett's and Bryant's weapons, still holstered to their sides.

Her cowboys guided her to the chair Emmett had just moved.

"Take a deep breath for us, Amber." Bryant's gentle command soothed her some.

"Her name is Kathy. Katherine White, to be exact." The man claiming to be her husband remained on his feet but didn't move an inch closer to her.

"It may be in that fucking report, but she'll always be Amber to me." Bryant's entire body seemed like a loaded weapon, safety off, finger on the trigger.

Mr. White's glances moved from Bryant and Emmett then back to her several times. He seemed cagey.

"I'm okay now," she told the Stone brothers, though her heartbeats sped up with each passing tick of the clock.

"Are you sure?" Bryant asked, holding her hand.

"Relax," she urged him, though doubting that, like her, either of her cowboys would be able to feel even the least little bit of ease at the moment.

"Do you recognize him, Amber?" Emmett's question didn't surprise her.

She turned to Emmett. He wasn't looking at her but was instead sending an icy stare Mr. White's way. If her cowboy's glare had been daggers, her presumed hubby would've been sliced to tiny bits.

She shook her head. "I remember nothing." Her big invisible wall remained fully intact, storing her memories on the other side, away from her conscious mind. "My name is Katherine?" she asked the stranger. "The report said 'Kathy.'"

"It is your legal name, honey. Kathy is a nickname."

"Usually a missing persons report uses a legal name and then lists nicknames." Jason Wolfe rubbed his chin.

"Typos I suppose, Sheriff. I'm so glad I found you, Kathy. I've been looking for you for some time. You can't imagine how scared I was you might be hurt or worse."

She studied his look, wondering if even a smidgen of her memory would return. He wore a black suit, which looked expensive, a black shirt, and a black tie.

*I'm not green right now. That's for sure.*

She guessed him to be in his late thirties, which seemed a little old for him to be her husband but not out of the realm of possibility. The guy's hair was thin, and his hairline went back too far on his head, making his forehead quite prominent. She could see streaks of gray hair on both sides of his temples. Where Emmett and Bryant were stunningly handsome, this man was at his best average. He wore a scraggily goatee that embellished his already-too-round face. His eyes were dull, lacking any deep color.

Had she really married this man? No emotions welled up inside her while she continued to examine his features. Nothing. Nada. Zilch.

"You can't imagine how hard this is for me, mister. I don't remember you." Her heart was breaking. How was she going to live in a future without her cowboys? It would kill her to say goodbye.

"You will, Kathy," Mr. White said. "There's no rush. Let me take you home tonight."

"Hold up, buddy." Emmett put his arm around her, which made the man frown, but she didn't care. It felt good to have her cowboy touch her. "She's not leaving Destiny until my brothers and I are certain you are who you say you are."

The guy turned to Sheriff Wolfe. "Are they in charge or are you?"

"Sit down, Mr. White. There's no rush, is there? You've found your wife, but she can't remember you. Let's take our time and see if you can jog her memory loose. Isn't that what we all want?"

Hearing not a single word from anyone to the sheriff's question, she didn't voice what she wished down to her very soul. She didn't want to remember anything. Letting her memories remain locked up behind the big wall was what she really hoped for. Her time at the cabin had increased her want for a future with Emmett, Bryant, and Cody. Not this guy, this man claiming to be married to her. On the other side of that wall were many unseen memories and other things, but not love. Love couldn't be contained by a mere wall, could it?

An older woman in a pink wig walked in carrying two folding chairs. "Sorry it took so long, Jason. These were in the back of the closet behind some boxes of files."

"Thanks, Shannon." The sheriff stepped from behind his desk and took the chairs. "If Officer Flowers or Officer Grinin calls, put them through, okay?"

"Will do, boss."

"Anyone else, just send them to my voice mail."

The woman left the room with a wink and a nod.

Sheriff Wolfe placed the chairs near the one she was sitting in. "Let's all have a seat and see what we can do to resolve this, okay?"

None of them moved to sit, but continued their silent, harsh stares at one another.

Mr. White didn't seem happy with the sheriff's idea, and he was definitely not thrilled with Emmett or Bryant's proximity to her. She didn't give a damn what the guy liked or didn't like. She wanted her cowboys near. They were the only ones who were keeping her sane in this crazy moment.

"Gentlemen, please take a seat," the sheriff pleaded once again.

"Yes, please," she added, hoping to grab onto a sliver of sanity for all of them.

Mr. White sat first. Then Bryant and Emmett did the same, scooting their folding chairs until they were touching hers on either side.

"Thank you, fellows." Jason looked her directly in the eyes. "Let's start again, shall we? Amber, I'm so pleased to finally get to meet you. I can't even picture how hard this has been for you."

The sheriff seemed kind to her, though also a man fixated on rules and order. He wasn't someone who tolerated chaos for long.

"I'm glad to meet you, too, Sheriff."

"What will help you right now? I know you don't remember

Sergei, but he's brought in your marriage license and a couple of pictures with you in them. One of the photos is the same one the Chicago PD sent to my office which I gave a copy of to Cody and Bryant."

"I saw it. It's me." She shook her head. How would she be able to live her life without her cowboys? Despair flattened her out completely.

"Do you have some questions for him?" the sheriff asked.

The image of the boy flashed in the back of her mind. "Yes, I do have questions for him. Do we have children?"

"We don't."

"The only person I can remember, and only glints of him, is a boy. He looks to be about eleven or twelve years old. I think he might be Hispanic. Dark hair, dark eyes. A cute kid. Do you know him?"

Mr. White pursed his lips out and shook his head. "Not a clue, Kathy. Sorry."

She watched Emmett's hands curl into fists. His words were harsh, like nails on a chalkboard. "You don't seem to know much at all, mister."

The stranger turned to Jason. "Nice little Podunk town you have here. Quite the welcome. These two may want to keep me and Kathy apart, but I will burn every building here to the ground before I let that happen."

Jason's eyebrows shot up and his fingertips touched the handle of his gun holstered to his side. "You think so?"

Sergei glared up at him but then held up his hands in what seemed to her like defiant resignation.

Amber needed to calm the tempers rising in this room. "Why was I driving my van here, Mr. White? Do you know where I was headed?"

"Call me Sergei, Kathy. Please." He leaned forward in his chair. "We live just outside Chicago. Your parents are in Arizona. I'm not sure how you got here. Central Northern Colorado is quite remote, babe. Maybe you got lost. It is the first time you've driven the trip alone."

"That doesn't even make sense." Bryant shot him a look of pure rage. "Not one fucking bit."

Emmett's hands were curled into fists. "Jason, have you done a Google search on her name? Does she have a Facebook account we can check?"

The sheriff nodded. "Too many Kathy Whites on Google. I found her on Facebook with Mr. White's help. He doesn't have an account and her page is set to let only friends see her personal information. Mrs. White, do you have any clue what your password is?"

She shook her head.

"I think we're rushing into this," Cody said. "Amber needs time to process."

"I don't give a damn what you or your brother think." The guy turned back toward the sheriff. "Speaking of the van, where is it? I'd like to recover my property as soon as possible."

"There's no way this bastard is Amber's husband." Bryant's sudden out-of-character outburst shocked her. "He's more concerned with a beat-up old van than about her well-being, Jason. Am I the only one who sees that?"

"Not the only one," Emmett added.

They were still trying to save her. They were going to fight for her. She loved them all so much.

"Fuck this. I came here to get Kathy. I don't need this bullshit, Sheriff." Sergei turned to her. "Kathy, let's go."

"Everyone needs to calm down right now," the sheriff stated flatly. His tone reminded her of how Emmett's had been back in the playroom.

"Tell me where my van is and Kathy and I will be out of your hair in a flash." Something about the way her so-called husband barked his words didn't sit right with her.

"Bryant and his brother found the van on County Road Twenty-

Two. Actually, it's not on the road but near it. From what they told me, where it landed, you'll need a big truck with a heavy-duty winch to retrieve it. I know a couple of guys who can help you out with that, Mr. White."

Sergei pulled out his cell and typed something into it. "County Road Twenty-Two. Got it." He tucked his phone back into the inner pocket of his suit coat. "Don't worry, Sheriff. I'll handle everything."

"Okay. Let me make myself clear, Mr. White. You may be her husband but you can't make her go with you," Jason informed. "She's an adult."

The man's face darkened. "But her mind is mixed up, Sheriff. She needs to come home with me. I'm sure her memory will return once she's back at our place."

"That might be so, but you still can't force her to leave."

Sergei leaned back in the chair. "I've got more pictures in my room at the hotel. Come with me, and I'll prove to you that you are my wife, Kathy."

"No way." Emmett's tone held a big dose of threat.

"Fuck, this is impossible," her supposed spouse said. "I'm not a guy who likes jumping through other people's hoops."

"What kind of guy are you? Enlighten us." Bryant wasn't playing around. One false move by White, and she was certain he would pulverize him with his fists.

"It might be a good start, Sergei," the sheriff said. "What do you do for a living?"

"This is ridiculous," the guy stated. "Fine. I'll jump for you. I'm an accountant. Boring, right? Maybe you don't understand why I want my van back, but money matters to me."

"And me? Do I matter to you, Sergei?" Calling him by name felt oddly familiar on her lips. Still no memory shot over the wall.

"Kathy, of course you do. We've been together almost three years now."

"Sergei, can't you understand why I'm hesitating to accept what you're saying? These guys have protected me ever since they found me. You might think they are being overly cautious, but I don't." They were heroes in her mind.

Mr. White nodded and his shoulders sagged slightly. "Of course, I understand. I'm just frustrated, Kathy. That's all. Wait. I did bring another picture with me. It's you and me together. I'm not sure I should show it to you or not. It might jog your memory too hard. Has she been seen by a doctor, Sheriff?"

Emmett's eyes narrowed. "We weren't able to come down from the mountain with her until now. The doctor just checked her out. She's fine. He called it retrograde amnesia. He says her memory could return at any time."

A thin smile spread across Sergei's unremarkable face. "I'm out of line here. You took care of my girl when she needed help. I should be thanking you two."

The man's sudden change of demeanor eased Amber's misgivings about him, but only a little. "Please show me the picture you brought with you."

"I will if you promise to at least eat dinner with me. I'm in a suite at the hotel. We could dine alone and talk everything out."

Before either Bryant or Emmett could decline his request, the sheriff held up his hand. "Wait, guys. I think these two do need to have some private time, but Mr. White, I think I have an idea that will satisfy all of us." Jason looked at her. "Amber, would you be open to having a meal with Sergei in a public place?"

"Yes."

The sheriff nodded his approval. "We have three places to choose from. There's Phong's Wok, Lucy's Burgers, or Blue's Diner. They're all located here in the square around Central Park."

"Hold on, Jason. I don't think this is a good idea." Bryant's hesitation was clearly shared by Emmett.

"Even if he is her husband as he states, that doesn't mean the rest of his story is true. What if Amber was running away from him? What if he was a terrible husband? I'm not leaving her alone with him until I know more, Jason," the older Stone brother added.

"I hear you both," the sheriff said. "I'm asking Mr. White to take her to one of the local eateries, but I'm also asking he sit in a table or booth, depending on where they choose to go, that is right by the window. That way you two can keep an eye on him right outside, and White and Amber can be alone. Make sense?"

"Fuck no," Bryant growled.

Amber grabbed his hand and then grabbed Emmett's with her other hand. "It's a good idea. I'll be okay. I'm not a little girl."

"Little girl or not, you're not going. Understand?" Emmett's throaty, forceful tone made her tremble—but not in the good way.

They were being overprotective, which she comprehended. Sergei was a stranger to them and to her, but he also could be telling the truth. What reason would he have for lying?

She needed them to trust her. "If anything goes wrong, I'll scream bloody murder until you come in to rescue me once again."

"Do we have a deal, guys, or not?" Mr. White stood.

"Let me see the picture you mentioned you'd brought with you first," she demanded.

His lips tightened into a thin line. "All right, Kathy."

Sergei reached into his coat opposite where he'd placed his cell. He extracted the photo and handed it to her.

She gazed at the image of her next to Sergei White. She was smiling and so was he.

"Do you remember anything about this?" Emmett asked, his anxious tone shaking her to the core.

The wall remained solid and foreboding, but a single thought shot over its crest and landed inside her head. "This was someone's birthday party, yes?" She looked up at Sergei, who was chewing on his lower lip.

He nodded. "Your twenty-fifth birthday, Kathy. Six months ago."

She closed her eyes, trying to pull more from the other side of the blockage. Nothing came. She opened her eyes and stared back at the photo she held in her hands. The image of the smile on her face slackened her apprehension about Sergei some.

"A public place will do just fine. Chinese sounds good to me," she said. "I've been living off sandwiches for way too long."

"I don't like this one damn bit, Amber." Bryant handed her his cell.

"Neither do I," Emmett added.

"Keep this with you." Bryant brushed the hair out of her eyes. "Promise me you'll call Emmett's cell if you need us for anything. He's number one on my speed dial."

"I promise I will, Bryant."

Emmett didn't move his stare from Sergei. "Amber, we'll be right outside watching Mr. White's every move."

"I've got nothing to hide." Mr. White pulled out his cell once again. "First, I need to let your parents know you're safe, Kathy." He typed a message into his phone. "All done. Let's go see what this pissant town has to offer."

* * * *

When Cody got back to the road after a full hour of climbing, he was still unhinged by what he'd found in the van.

Had Amber been driving it when she had her accident? As much as he believed she'd fallen from heaven onto the ranch by some kind of act of fate, he knew better. She was flesh and blood. A real woman. The van had to be the vehicle she'd been in. There was no other explanation he could come up with no matter how much he wanted another. Perhaps she'd been a passenger, even a hostage. He clung to that idea, no matter how far-fetched or how horrible to think, with every fiber of his being. If true, Amber was no longer a hostage of whatever creep had held her. She was safe now. If not, he prayed Amber's memories would never return. Let her dark past remain a mystery to her. That would be best for her, and for him and his brothers.

He looked over at his horse, still tied to the tree twenty feet from the drop-off. "Good, boy." Tuxedo's ears were up, and his nostrils were flaring. "Settle down. Sorry I left you so long."

Catching his breath from the hard climb back up the cliff, he looked at the horizon. The sun had already dipped below it, but there was still just enough light in the sky that he didn't have to bring out the flashlight.

Before heading Tuxedo's direction, he scanned the items he'd brought up the cliff. His jaw clenched once again. These weren't good for Amber. Not one damn bit. Not good for any of them.

The purse held Amber's driver's license. Once again, he looked at her picture. God, she was beautiful. Twenty-five years old, turning twenty-six in another month. Her name was Katherine White. That didn't fit her in his mind. She would be "Amber" forever to him.

The bag also had a slip of paper he thought might help solve the mystery, though he was worried what more he would discover if he continued pursuing the truth. But he knew he must. Whatever more he found about Amber, she was his woman, and he would not let past sins take her away from him no matter what. On the note were a name and a phone number. Nate Wright. Did that guy have anything to do with the other items he'd found in the van? How was Amber mixed up with him? The area code was the same as Destiny's, which meant the man was in Colorado, but that could be anywhere from the entire Western border—Durango to Steamboat Springs—and the whole northern third of the state. Once bars appeared back on his cell's service indicator, he planned on calling Mr. Wright. If the dude ever had done anything that hurt her or put her in danger, Cody would kill the son of a bitch.

Another perplexing item was the registration he'd found in the compartment in the dashboard. The van belonged to the Green Lakes Boys' Home in Chicago, not Amber. Was the van stolen? Another call to make once his fucking phone was working again.

The last item was unfathomable to him. He'd brought up only this plastic bag, leaving the other two identical in every way to this one, including contents. Still shocked by the packages, he held this one up to take another look. It resembled broken glass, but he had no doubt it was crystal meth. His gut tightened.

What the hell was Amber doing with all those drugs? None of it made any sense to him. He needed to get to her fast. She was in trouble, and he wasn't about to let her face that without him. No one would harm her or take her away from him—not even the law, should they come looking for her. Whatever her past held, he would stand by her side and keep her safe. He believed his brothers would, too.

She'd cracked his ever-so-serious and always-dutiful brother's walls. Emmett was changed. Bryant, too, was different. His twin had thrown caution to the wind and had fallen hard for Amber. *And me? What about me?* He'd been looking for so long, dreaming of a day when they could be a real family again—he and his brothers sharing, adoring, and loving a woman together. Amber was the love of his life. She was the one.

He heard a crack of a branch behind him, and his survival training kicked into gear. Tuxedo had been trying to warn him in his way that they weren't alone, but he'd been too tired and too stupid to realize it.

Dropping his packages from the van to the ground, he ducked and spun around.

His move kept him from being hit over the head with a metal pipe.

Cody balled up his left hand and punched his attacker in the nuts, while freeing his pistol from its holster with his right hand.

Out of the corner of his eye, Cody spotted another man, pointing a thirty-eight his direction.

The man with the pipe crumpled to the ground with a thud.

With no hesitation, Cody emptied five of his gun's bullets into the other man's chest.

*Bang. Bang. Bang. Bang. Bang.*

The creep got off a single shot that hit him in his left leg.

He remained low, scanning every direction for any other assholes that might have come with these two.

He found no one else.

Straightening up, he pointed the barrel of his gun at the guy he'd turned into a eunuch.

He scanned the other prick he'd filled with lead. Dead as a doornail.

He limped closer to the other man. "Who the fuck sent you? Nate Wright?"

# Chapter Fourteen

Amber looked out the big picture window at Bryant and Emmett standing by the dragon statue that guarded the southwest corner of the park in the center of Destiny. Around the green space were the four roads that made up the city's square and housed most of its business.

Knowing her cowboys were across the road, just on the other side of South Street, gave her some comfort. They'd never stopped glaring through the window of Phong's Wok at the man who had come to take her away from Destiny.

Sergei stood by the stone Buddha near the front door, talking on his cell and glancing back at her several times. This was the fourth time he'd taken or made a call. He'd apologized each time, claiming the calls were work related.

She looked at her plate of orange chicken, which she'd only taken a couple of bites from. Her appetite had vanished the moment she'd walked into the sheriff's office earlier. She was thirsty, but her glass of water had been empty for over fifteen minutes. There'd been no sign of staff or owners coming to their table with a pitcher. In fact, there was no sign of staff anywhere to be found. Even the customers had disappeared right after Mr. White and she arrived. Very strange, but a quick look at her cell told her that the current time—3:31—had to be a downtime around Destiny. Right this minute, she and White were in between the lunch rush and the dinner crowd.

Sergei sat back down at their table. "Okay. Where were we?"

"At the very beginning. How did you and I meet?"

"Why do you insist on grilling me like a two-bit criminal?" His angry tone was easy to detect.

“I’m sorry if my questions are making you feel that way. That’s not my intention.”

He rolled his eyes, and she felt a heavy pit in her gut. “You said you remembered a boy. Do you recall his name?”

She shook her head. “I wish I did. He seems so lost and sweet.”

“Hispanic, right?”

“That’s right.”

“Let’s toss around some common Spanish boys’ names, Kathy. Maybe one of them will unlock your mind.”

“Okay. Maybe it will.”

“Let’s start with the letter *J*, shall we?”

“Sure thing,” she answered but wondered why he’d chosen the middle of the alphabet as opposed to the beginning.

Several that began with the letter *A* came to her mind. Alberto. Alfonzo. Antonio. Many more popped in her head but none of them were the boy’s name, of that she was certain.

“Let’s begin,” White said. “Jesus. Javier. Jose.”

“No. None of those sound right to me.” She closed her eyes and brought up the image of the boy in the back of her mind. The kid’s smile was so sweet. Who was he?

“Look at me, Kathy.” Sergei’s tone seemed to carry a suspicious note to Amber. Or was that just her overactive imagination getting the best of her?

She opened her eyes and looked directly into White’s. She watched him squeeze his eyes tight and, as before, chew on his lower lip. Silent alarms were firing inside her, but she wasn’t sure why. She had the oddest urge to wave Bryant and Emmett inside. Why? What reason would she be able to tell her cowboys if she motioned them in? That she didn’t like his tone? No way. Sergei might actually be telling the truth, and where did that leave her?

When White opened his eyes back up after what felt like at minimum a full minute to her, she watched his face cloud up with what seemed to her to be anger and volatility. She leaned back in her chair, trying to put an extra inch of space between them. Silly? Maybe, but she needed to be cautious.

He tapped his fingers on the table, creating a *rat-tat-tat* repetitive sound. Then he grabbed her hand. “What about ‘Juan’ for the boy’s name? You think that’s his name?”

She pulled her hand free from his grasp. Maybe she’d liked his touch in her former life, but right now, right here, she definitely didn’t. Everything inside her was recoiling from Sergei, but she wasn’t sure why or even if it was appropriate. How could she trust her gut when her head had taken a hike, leaving no forwarding address?

Sergei reached across the table and cupped her chin. Then he glanced out the window. He knew Bryant and Emmett were within a couple of leaps from them. Her cowboys.

His cell buzzed again. White looked at the screen and frowned. “I’ve got to take this, Kathy.”

“It’s fine, Sergei. Take your call.”

He stepped back to the place he’d been standing in before. He talked quietly into his cell, so quiet she couldn’t make out any of his words.

She placed her chopsticks on the side of her plate. No more bites. She felt completely frustrated by how this day had turned out. She thought about looking back at Bryant and Emmett, but she couldn’t right now. It would be much too painful, but more pain was heading her way. Sergei meant for her to go with him back to their home outside Chicago. She closed her eyes and tried to bring up anything about the place. Nothing. The only space that came back was the playroom in the brothers’ cabin. She crunched her eyelids even tighter. The picture of her and Sergei floated to the front of her mind. White had told her it had been taken at her birthday party. That didn’t feel right to her. Yes, it was a birthday party, but it wasn’t hers. Then whose? The face of the sweet boy glided on the surface of her consciousness, next to the invisible wall. Was the party where the photo had been taken for him? For Juan?

Juan. Juan Garcia. She remembered. It was his twelfth birthday. She'd put it together for him in the main room of the boys' home where she worked. She opened her eyes and felt the tears of recollection roll down her cheek. She visualized the wall, which had kept her memories locked away since her accident, crumbling into dust and then vanishing from her mind forever.

Like a flood, everything she'd forgotten came crashing back into her consciousness. Her name was Kathy White, just as Sergei had told her. But his last name wasn't "White," and he wasn't her husband. He was her boss. Sergei Mitrofanov was the director of the Green Lakes Boys' Home right in the heart of Chicago. She was the resident therapist for the place. The home was part of a network of homes for orphans, which were founded and funded by an anonymous philanthropist. What would he think if he knew one of his boys' homes was fronting a drug dealer?

Her mind slipped back to the moment that had changed everything for her.

*Kathy looked out her window into the parking lot at Juan, standing next to his bike. She wondered why he was out there by himself. The boys usually rode their bikes together, which was encouraged by the entire staff, including her. It was important that the boys' bonds grew. They were family. They needed each other.*

*She was about to head down the hall and go outside and ask him when she spotted Sergei out of the corner of her eye through her window. The director walked up to Juan and towered over him. She couldn't hear what he was saying, but she could see the boy's trembling hands. Whatever Sergei was telling him frightened Juan.*

*Her mouth dropped as she saw the director reach in his suit coat and pull out a piece of paper and a plastic bag filled with what looked to her to be some kind of drug. Juan tucked the bag into his backpack before riding off on his bike.*

*Two emotions tied her up in a knot—disgust and fear. The first was for her sleazeball boss. The latter was for Juan.*

*She wasn't sure what to do to get Juan out of harm's way. She bolted to her car, passing right by the asshole.*

*"What's wrong, Kathy?"*

*"Family emergency, Sergei," she blurted, surprising herself.*

*Unfortunately, it took her two hours to locate Juan. She found him in a park a mile from Green Lakes. He sat in a swing, staring down at his feet.*

*"Juan," she shouted.*

*He looked up and leapt to his feet. He ran to his bike, which was leaning against the wall near the swing set. She ran as fast as she could and got to him before he could escape.*

*Big tears fell from his brown eyes.*

*"Lo siento. Por favor, perdóname." Though he spoke fluent Spanish, Juan mostly spoke English to her. Whenever he didn't, she knew something was wrong. Really wrong.*

*"It's okay, Juan. I'm here. Tell me what happened to the plastic bag Mr. Mitrofanov gave you in the parking lot."*

*"I obeyed Mr. Mitrofanov, Ms. White. I took the bag to the address on the paper he gave me. Two men took it from me and gave me this money." He reached into his backpack and pulled out two fat rolls of hundred-dollar bills.*

*She wasn't about to count it here, but knew the stash had to be several thousand dollars. Her blood boiled hot. Sergei was using Juan to transport drugs to dealers. His dealers? Which of the other boys was the asshole forcing to do the same? She wouldn't be surprised if he was using all of them.*

*Juan rubbed his eyes, swollen from crying. "I know I shouldn't have done it, Ms. White, but Mr. Mitrofanov told me he would kick me out of Green Lakes if I didn't do what he wanted me to do."*

*"This isn't your fault, Juan." Unsure what her next move should be, she took him to her sister's place, which was in Katy, a full hour away from Sergei and the boys' home.*

*Belle gave Juan a glass of milk and a plate of cookies. Her nursing skills weren't needed today, but her sister did know how to ease a troubled boy's guilt.*

*"Kathy, here's Nate Wright's number." Belle pushed the paper across the table. "I don't know him myself, but I know people who do. He's the sheriff up in Bliss, Colorado, and I believe he can help bring your goddamn boss down for good. Nate knows more about drug dealers than either of us ever will."*

*She called Nate right then, hoping her sister was right about him. Their conversation was brief.*

*Wright's voice came through loud and clear. "Without evidence, it will be next to impossible to convict this guy."*

*"But I saw him give Juan the plastic bag."*

*"Darlin', if I hauled in everyone who passed around a plastic bag, the jails would be full. You have no proof. Honestly, even if you had held the bag in your hand and inspected it, unless you managed to get a sample, we couldn't be sure. You believe it was crystal meth, but you're not a chemist and Juan's twelve, so I'm sure he isn't either. Though now that I think about it, we got a couple of teenaged evil geniuses here, so I shouldn't judge. The Farley boys are going to run a crime syndicate one of these days. If they don't blow up the town first."*

*Wright had a deep, laid-back Western accent and seemed to be willing to go off subject. She had to pull him back in. "So there's no way to convict him?"*

*He chuckled over the line, a deep, almost soothing sound. "Now there's always a way to convict someone. I suggest you head to Bliss, Kathy. I'll make a few calls and see what I can find out about Mr. Mitrofanov. I used to be in the DEA. I still have some contacts there. You'll find out we never say 'die' here in Bliss. Well, not when it comes to solving a problem, that is. We're actually the murder capital of the country, so we say 'die' a whole lot."*

*The lawman's words weren't convincing her that there was any chance Sergei would be convicted. "If I could bring you a couple bags of the dope to see for yourself, would that help our case against him?"*

*"That's not a good idea. Come to Bliss and let's talk about this. You need to stay away from that boys' home."*

*But she couldn't do that. The other boys were still in jeopardy as long as Sergei remained free and able to run Green Lakes. If Nate needed evidence to build an open-and-shut case, she would find it.*

*Later, after two in the morning, she parked her car in front of the boys' home. The admin building was empty, unlike the home's dormitory, which housed fifty-two orphaned youngsters, who were hopefully all asleep. She walked down the hallway to Sergei's office in the dark. She wasn't about to turn on a light and alert Marcus, the staffer who had worked nights here for more than ten years.*

*Even though she knew Sergei's office door must be locked, she still tried to turn its handle, but it didn't budge. She opened her purse and peered at its contents—a little makeup, her wallet, the paper with Nate's contact information, and her universal tool she never left home without. The admin building was the oldest on the property. Every door, including this one, had big gaps between the door and frame. She twisted the screwdriver into the gap where the bolt mechanism sat. It worked to release the lock. She swung the director's door wide. The light from the streetlamp shining through the window was enough illumination. In less than five minutes, she found three plastic bags filled with more dope in an unlocked drawer of his filing cabinet. The arrogant fucker apparently wasn't afraid of ever being caught. How long had he been using the boys to work his criminal activity? He'd been director here for quite some time, long before she'd been hired.*

*She scooped the bags up in her arms. She would take these to Bliss and hand them over to Nate. Sergei would go down and the sweet, innocent boys here would be safe.*

*Suddenly Sergei's office brightened up from the headlights shining through his window. She peered out the blinds and saw the asshole getting of his car, which he'd parked next to hers. Terror made her mouth desert dry and her pulse lightning fast.*

*Instead of going out the front to her car, she ran to the back of the building, pulling the keys to the home's van from the hook by the back door. The tiny parking lot was much smaller than the one out front. Of the four parking spaces back here, only one had her last escape option—the Green Lake Boys' Home's white van.*

A little more than a week ago, Amber had left Chicago for Bliss, Colorado, not Destiny. But the confusing roads mixed with her overwrought state caused her to take at least one wrong turn, maybe two. When she was stopped by a flat tire on the van, she'd started out on foot in search of help. After walking for only God knew how long, the wind had started picking up. The storm was rolling in. She'd tripped and hit her head on a fallen log. The next thing she remembered was being in the cabin with her three amazing cowboys.

As the memory faded away, Amber's heart thumped hard and fast in her chest.

She looked at the lying bastard still talking on his phone. Sergei's back was to her, so she chanced a quick look out the window, but the two men she expected to wave inside Phong's were no longer standing by the dragon statue. Her heart leapt into her throat. Where were they?

With the cell still glued to his ear, Sergei glanced at her for a second, inducing a horrific cold shiver inside her.

She forced her lips to reshape into a smile, realizing it would be in her best interest to continue to play dumb with her old boss if she had any chance of getting out of this mess.

When Sergei turned back to face the wall and let her get a view of his back, Amber quickly typed a text to Emmett and prayed he would get it. She also sent a text message to Cody, even though she bet he was still on the mountain without cell service.

Her eyes darted around the restaurant, which was strangely empty, save her and Sergei. Where were the waitresses? The other customers? What had her old boss done? Something to ensure he could be alone with her?

Another hasty glance out the window pulverized her completely. With her memories back and no sign of her rescuers' whereabouts, a bad omen took hold of her, dimming whatever light might've been at the end of this bloody tunnel. She still wasn't going to give up without a fight, but she wanted to be smart.

Before she could risk another text, Sergei walked back to the table.

He laughed. "Got your memory back, Kathy?"

"No, Mr. White. I don't," Amber lied, hating the shakiness she heard in her voice.

"Time to end this charade, don't you think?" His murderous stare was horrifying to see.

"Maybe we should call it a day for now. We can pick this up in the morning."

"Don't try to fuck me over again, Kathy. I saw the panic in your eyes when you looked around this dump. Don't worry. I didn't come to town alone. I brought some of my guys with me. A couple of them tied up the staff and put them in the freezer out back after we were served our food. Four more have been making sure no one, not even those two idiots across the street, comes in for moo goo gai pan."

The man was evil and completely nuts.

"I don't know what you're talking about, Mr. White."

"You know my name is Mitrofanov. Stop bullshitting me and maybe I will spare your little wetback." The hollowness of her old boss terrified her.

"While you were on the phone, I left a message for Emmett to come get me."

He pulled out a gun from inside his jacket. He pointed the barrel at her chest. "Do you take me for a fool, Kathy?" His tone burned her like acid.

"I don't know what to think about you anymore," she confessed. "I thought I knew you, but I was wrong."

"Know this, Kathy, my men are making sure the sheriff and those two cowboys are out of commission. I didn't come to this fucking town alone. I'm not an idiot."

"Why, Sergei? I can't understand how you got caught up in the drug business and pulled the boys in with you."

"Money. Simple as that, babe. Where is Juan?"

Clearly, Sergei hadn't found the boy, thank God. "Safe."

He slapped her in the face hard. She brought her fingers up to her nose, which was bleeding.

"You thought you would get enough shit on me to put me behind bars, right? That's why you took my product from my office. My guys will do whatever it takes to get those bags back in my hands. A couple of them are on it right now."

"What do you want me to say, Sergei?" Had all she'd done been for nothing? At least Juan was safe, but for how long?

"You and I will be leaving this hellhole in about ten minutes. Once I get you back to my place, I'll figure out a way to get you to tell me where the boy is. I've got several ideas rolling through my head already about how to accomplish that."

"You don't want to do that, Sergei. Those cowboys you met in the sheriff's office won't stop looking for me. Trust me."

She heard what sounded like either a car backfiring several times—or gunshots.

"Your bumpkins are all dead by now."

Overwhelmed by dread, she wanted to scream, to claw Sergei's eyes out, to crawl into a hole and sob until her own life expired. Had she unknowingly led this monster to Destiny, to her cowboys? This bastard didn't know them the way she did. The Stone brothers were survivors. They couldn't be dead. They just couldn't.

"Kathy, the mess you created wasn't something I planned for, but I do know how to clean up such things. Without evidence and without witnesses, there is no case, babe. Last chance, Kathy, to make things easier for you." He pushed the tip of his gun between her eyes. "Where is Juan?"

Sergei's cell buzzed. He stepped back, removing the steel off of her. "Fuck. Dimitri, too. *Vzdohr.*" His face darkened. "*Gdye* the sheriff? *Da.* How far is that? We'll be long gone by the time he gets back after we take care of the rest of our business. Any word from the two we sent to get our product back?"

*The drugs.* If Sergei ever looked away, she would run for the exit.

"*Niet.* You sure those cowboys didn't see the rest of you? Good. These cowboys want to play Wild West, let's give them our kind of showdown. Six to two are odds I'm always ready to take them. Counting me, seven to two." His frown returned. "There's another cowboy who showed up?"

Amber's heart leapt up in her chest. Bryant and Emmett were okay. Cody likely was still up the road from Destiny. Her cowboys were safe.

"*Da.* Seven to three. Still good odds. Position you and your men on the roofs around the park. *Da.* Hurry but don't worry. You'll have time enough. I have their kryptonite." Sergei put his cell back in his inner pocket. His evil grin sent a horrible shiver down her spine, chilling her bones. "Get up, Kathy. We're going to take a walk."

# Chapter Fifteen

Bryant's leg was bleeding and possibly fractured.

The cause? The four bastards who'd jumped him and Emmett by the statue.

Emmett had perceived the fuckers before he had, since the thugs had come up on their right, same side as his brother's good ear. In a flash, Emmett had taken out one of the creeps straight away.

That had left three.

The goons had been armed, but so had he and his brother. Before any of their assailants could get off even a single shot, he and Emmett had shot several rounds into each of them.

He and his brother pointed their thirty-eights at the only man still conscious of the group. The punk had lost his gun when Emmett, the best shot in the family by far, had nailed him in the shoulder.

The asshole glared at them, keeping his hand on the wound his brother had given him. "Go fuck yourselves, faggots."

"Don't be a dumb-ass, dude." Emmett's barrel was pointed right between the man's eyes.

"I'd listen to him if I were you," he told the dick on the ground. "My brother holds the highest marksmanship badges in the Marine Corps for both rifle and pistol. The only reason you're still alive is my brother wanted you to be."

"I'm not saying a fucking thing until I see my lawyer."

Eric Knight came up beside him, carrying his Glock. "Asshole, do they look like the law to you?"

Eric and his brother Scott weren't typical wealthy assholes—and boy, were they loaded. Billionaires, even. They had created and continued to run one of the most lucrative online gaming sites in the world, but they were still cowboys, just like their dads.

Eric turned to them. “Heard all the gunfire. You guys have caused quite the disturbance.”

As if on cue, more of Destiny’s citizens appeared around them, all packing.

Eric turned back to the man on the ground. “Be smart, dude. Make it easy on yourself and answer my friend’s questions.”

Bryant tried to keep his cool. “Tell us why you’re here and who you’re after.”

“Not a chance,” the asshole snarled.

“Are you thinking what I’m thinking?” Bryant asked Emmett.

“If you’re thinking this motherfucker is too stupid to live, then, yes, I am.” With his free hand, Emmett punched the asshole in the face as hard as he could.

The prick’s nose bled like a spigot. The hate in his eyes seemed to swap places with fear. Not as stupid as he looked. Now, they were getting somewhere.

“You’ve really pissed off my brother, dude. Not good. I’ll ask you again, nicely. Why are you here?”

“He’s here for Amber.” Cody came up beside him, limping.

“What the fuck happened to your leg?” Emmett asked.

“I could ask Bryant the same question, but I can see for myself you guys also had a run-in with your own set of assholes.”

Glad to have his twin with him, Bryant said, “Lead pipe. My leg might be broken.”

“I took out my pipe-carrying dick. The one with the gun got me. Flesh wound. Just a scratch. Gun-prick is dead, but pipe-guy is tied up next to the rockslide above the van. Amber’s in trouble, and I mean big trouble. Her real name is Kathy White. There’s more to tell, but…” Cody’s eyes narrowed. “Where is she?”

“Phong’s,” he said.

“Go,” Eric said. “The rest of us will take care of these assholes.”

Bryant nodded, and bolted back to the woman of his dreams, ignoring the pain in his leg.

He and Emmett had been distracted by the ambush from their most important assignment, keeping an eye on Amber, keeping her safe.

Having two good, uninjured legs, Emmett ran a little ahead of him and Cody to where they all prayed *she* was still sitting, bright-eyed and beautiful as ever.

* * * *

Tearing down South Street faster than he'd ever run, even during his tour in Iraq, Emmett was swamped by guilt. His fuckup had put Amber in danger. The second he saw Sergei, the hairs on the back of his neck had stood up. He'd known better than to give in to Amber's rebellion, insisting to go to dinner with the fucker. Now she was alone with the psychopath, all because he'd consented. *Fuck.* He silently cursed himself as his feet ate up more of the pavement.

One block left.

He and his brothers were running, holding their loaded thirty-eights with their fingers on the triggers, which was a blatant disregard for normal safety guidelines. But this wasn't normal or safe. None of them gave a fuck about anyone's safety save one, Amber, their woman.

Rounding the corner and less than twenty feet from Phong's, he and his brothers hit the brakes when he saw his love held by Sergei, who also held a gun to her head.

"Here is your *troika*, Kathy. Right on time, too." The lunatic twisted his lips into a sneer.

Amber's nose was bleeding onto her upper lip, enraging him to the very edge of his control. "Guys, he's—"

Sergei slapped his hand over her mouth, silencing her, but kept her in front of him, crouching behind her like a coward. "*Niet*, my love. No talking."

His heart pounded against his ribs like a wrecking ball. "I got this," he whispered to his brothers. "Distract him and I'll get the shot."

"Deal," Cody whispered back. "Take down the bastard."

His brothers knew his sharpshooting skills surpassed theirs by far. They wouldn't risk a chance of missing the fucker and hitting Amber. They would trust him to slay Sergei and save Amber. His gut tightened, knowing that even with his expertise, there was still a risk. This whole fucking thing was wrought with risks as long as the motherfucker held a gun and their woman. As horrific as Iraq's many war zones had been, he'd never felt a more agonizing burden than now. One shot and this nightmare could be over, or could go on and on for the rest of his life.

Cody took a step left, away from him. Bryant did the same to the right.

"Stop right there, cowpokes. I'm not stupid. You move another inch and I put a bullet in Kathy's pretty head."

*Come on, fucker. Show me your face.*

But he didn't. The fucker was no better than the goddamn Taliban. More than once, he'd seen them use innocents—women and children—marching them in front of their worthless asses as cover.

*One little peek over her shoulder, Sergei. Just one.*

"You want your drugs, right?" Cody asked. "Let her go and I will take you to them."

"I've got men retrieving my product already."

"Really?" Cody held up a bag. "This look familiar to you? Your boys aren't coming down *our* mountain anytime soon, mister."

Sergei cursed in Russian, but he still didn't come out from behind Amber.

"We took out the other four in town, Sergei." Bryant's tone shredded the very air. Gone was his quiet restraint. Amber had changed him, changed them all.

*Come on, you motherfucking coward.*

Amber's eyes were darting madly.

"Three big weapons against my little pistol. Doesn't seem fair to me."

She kept looking up, past them, and then back.

*Up?* Sergei must have more men.

"On the roofs," he whispered to his brothers.

After that, everything happened simultaneously and lightning fast.

Cody and Bryant crouched, twisted around, and started blasting away.

Amber balled up her fist and hit Sergei in the groin.

His grasp on her didn't hold.

She crouched to the ground.

The madman's face was twisted in pain, then shock, as he realized his shield was gone.

*Clear shot!*

Emmett unloaded every bullet into the man's head, making hamburger out of his brains. He tried to run to Amber, but fell to the ground instead.

Agonizing pain, unimaginable and overwhelming, seemed to permeate every inch of his body, but especially in his chest.

He needed to get up, to go to Amber, to cover her with his body from the barrage of bullets, to make sure she was safe.

More gunshots.

"Fuck!" he shouted, ignoring the pain and willing himself to his feet. He couldn't focus his eyes, but moved in the direction he knew *she* was.

Still gripping his gun, he took a single step and fell again. *Please, God, let her be okay.*

Readying himself for another attempt to get upright, he closed his eyes, paying no attention to the crushing pangs in his chest.

He felt familiar fingers on his face. Amber. "Emmett? Oh God. No." Her panicky words blew away his despair.

*She's alive.*

"He's been shot." Bryant's serious tone didn't worry him any. Thank God, she was okay.

He tried to speak, but could only grunt. The pain he'd backed down moments ago by sheer will returned with a vengeance.

"Don't try to sit up, Emmett." Cody was alive and kicking.

His heart had never felt such relief, such joy.

He opened his eyes, forcing them to focus. Luckily, this time they obeyed, and he saw his family—Bryant, Cody, and *her*, Amber, their woman.

The looks in his brothers' eyes were too familiar. He'd seen it in combat in the troubled stares of fellow soldiers gathered around the fallen.

He resigned himself that this was it, his time. He was dying.

A calmness, warm and sleepy, billowed inside him.

Amber was crying.

He reached for her hand.

She wrapped her fingers in his. "Talk to me. What do you want, Emmett? What do you need?"

Need and want? Simple. More time with her. Much more. War was hell and fate had chosen this moment for his exit. But she was alive and safe. He had no doubt his brothers would make certain she stayed that way.

He wanted to tell her that everything was going to be okay. He needed to let her know how much he loved her. But his throat wasn't cooperating.

Emmett stared at her beautiful face, and then the world began to spin. Faster and faster.

"He's passing out." Cody's voice sounded so remote.

Even more, Bryant's words were distant, faraway, beyond the horizon. "Compress his wound with both hands."

"Please. Don't leave me, Emmett. Stay with me. Oh God." Amber's sobs faded into the vast empty space he was plunging into.

*My brothers will take care of you, little one. Good-bye, my love.*

Spiraling down, down, down…

* * * *

Calling on his field training, Cody continued compressing Emmett's chest wound, harder during his inhalations and softer during his exhalations. The biggest risk now for his brother was a collapsed lung.

He looked over at Amber, who was in a state of shock. All the color in her face was gone.

"Sweetheart, listen to me. He's still breathing. I don't need you passing out on me, too. Understand?"

No answer. Her eyes remained wide with horror.

He harshened his tone. "Slave, answer me. Do. You. Understand?"

"Yes, Sir," she said in a wispy tone, coming back to him, if only a little.

"That's my girl. Hang tough. I need you to be strong, little one."

"I'll try, Master."

Bryant had left to find Doc Ryder and bring him back.

Cody had seen his fair share of wounds like his brother's in Afghanistan. Thankfully, the bullet hadn't exited out Emmett's back. If it had, his brother wouldn't have a chance, not that he was out of the woods yet.

Scott Knight ran up to him. "Doc's on his way, Cody. Should be here in five minutes."

He nodded. "Would you take Amber someplace else?"

"No," she snapped firmly, a hint her haze was lifting some. "I'm not leaving Emmett."

"Okay, baby. You can stay." He looked at Knight. "Make sure she doesn't fall down."

"Sure thing." The billionaire brother put his arm around her.

"How about we sit down, miss."

"Okay," she muttered, glancing back at the corpse of Sergei, the motherfucker Emmett had nailed in the head with every bullet from his pistol. Securely on the ground, she took a deep breath. "Emmett's going to make it."

"Yes, little one." He prayed it was true.

His big brother had saved Amber—their woman. Emmett had always been his hero, though Cody couldn't think of a time he'd ever told him.

Even though they were tight, as tight as any brothers could be, he'd resented Emmett trying to step up and play parent after the accident that took their mom and dads. The sacrifices his brother made had been colossal. Placing two orphaned fifteen-year-olds together in a foster home wasn't going to happen. If Emmett hadn't cast his dreams of college aside to make sure he and Bryant stayed together with him, their family would've been ripped apart even more.

More of Destiny's citizens filled the street. He watched as Hiro and Melissa Phong led their staff out onto the street. They all seemed to be unharmed. He noticed several people offer the shivering employees their jackets. He'd been around the world during his years in the service, but no place on earth was like this place. Neighbors helped each other without fail.

Cody felt a hand on his back. He turned and looked into the loving eyes of Ethel, the wife of Patrick and Sam O'Leary. Though there was no genetic connection, she and her husbands were like grandparents to him and his brothers.

The silver-haired lady's blue eyes sparkled with apparent hope. "Cody, he's going to be okay. You'll see."

Standing next to her, Patrick agreed. "Ethel's right. Have faith."

He nodded and looked back at Emmett. Faith. More than his big brother or even Bryant, he'd been labeled as having too much of it. The day Amber had arrived, his beliefs in the possible mushroomed high into the sky. Now, he needed faith, faith for his brother, his hero.

He leaned down and whispered into Emmett's ear, choking back doubt. "Fate brought Amber to us to make us a family again. You've got to fight. Fight, Emmett. Believe in us. I sure believe in you."

# Chapter Sixteen

Emmett continued spiraling down, but the spinning and the descent seemed to be slowing. Death wasn't what he'd imagined, not that he'd given it much thought before. Afterlife issues were Cody's to mull over, not his.

No fire yet. He took that as a good sign, knowing the list was incredibly long that had earned him a ticket to the brimstone burg. He'd killed while in the Marine Corps. Duty to his country demanded his best, and he'd given it. He didn't revel in his kills in Iraq. He did, however, take great satisfaction for one kill, his last. If the Devil's playground was his final destination, he would be sure to look up Sergei, the motherfucker who had meant to harm his Amber. That would definitely bring a little heaven to his eternity.

"He's smiling." Amber didn't sound distant or dreamlike. "Emmett, are you awake?"

Was he still on the ground in the middle of the street? He never expected to hear her sweet voice again. The pain returned but duller than before. He opened his eyes and gazed at the love of his life's beautiful, concerned face.

"I'm here, cowboy." Amber pressed her lips to his. He could feel heaven and earth and everything in between in that kiss.

"You put quite the scare in us, bro." Leaning on crutches, Cody stood next to Amber. "How's your pain?"

"Bearable. Pain meds?"

"Yes," Bryant said in his familiar smooth, unflappable tone. He was also on crutches.

"How's the leg?"

"Broke." His brother lifted his leg to show him the cast. "I'll have this for a couple of months."

He would be okay. That's all that mattered. "And what about you, Cody? You said it was only a flesh wound."

"It is. Doc just wants me to have these for a few days." Normally light and sarcastic, Cody's tone grew serious and warm. "Emmett, glad you're back."

"Me, too, bro." Emmett looked back at Amber. "Me, too."

"More importantly, how are you feeling?" his sweet baby asked.

"I've been better." He looked into Amber's golden eyes and saw his future.

"*Hola, señor*." A young boy peered from behind her. "Thank you for saving Miss White."

"My pleasure." Emmett turned to Amber. "The boy from your dreams?"

She nodded. "Emmett Stone, I'd like to introduce you to Juan Garcia."

Emmett shook the boy's hand. "Pleased to meet you, Juan."

"*Mucho gusto, Señor* Stone."

"Juan, give Mr. Stone some breathing room." A very nice-looking, fair-haired woman stood by the door, behind Cody and Bryant. "Come back over here to me."

Amber smiled at the woman. "Emmett, this is my sister, Belle. Sis, come meet my guy."

"Later, Kat. He needs his rest." Belle glanced around the small room. "There are already way too many people in here if you ask me. You and his brothers make three. Juan and I are four and five. And Nate is six."

Amber shrugged. "My sister is a nurse and a stickler about rules, Emmett. I had to threaten her within an inch of her life to stay in here until you woke up."

Emmett looked at Belle, who had her arm around Juan. "She's tough looking, but my money will always be on you in a fair fight."

Amber rewarded him with a lovely grin, and nothing in the world could be as beautiful.

And Emmett had almost lost her. He struggled to remember what happened after he'd been shot. "How about filling me in about what happened after Sergei hit the dirt?"

"That's my cue," a dark-headed man with blue eyes said, offering his hand.

Emmett shook it. "You are?"

"Sheriff Nate Wright. Your woman's sister knew a friend of mine and put us in touch." The sheriff's cell rang. "Damn it. One sec." He put the phone up to his ear. "Hey, baby. What's up? What do you mean? Have you called Doc?" Whatever the gal on the other side of the conversation was saying had caused a frown to be plastered on his face. "How the hell did Charlie ruin my Stetson? I thought you said he was just teething. What do you mean teething babies sometimes throw up? Okay. But why did it have to be my Stetson? Why do my boys have to puke or poop on everything I own? Seriously, Callie, I'm down to two shirts and now my second-best hat is gone. No, I can't wear it again. Put him on. Hey, Zane. I just want you to know that the next time I'm changing Charlie or Zander, I fully intend to use your autographed Rangers cap as a peepee teepee. I know you aimed him at my hat. I'll be home as quick as I can wrap up things here in Destiny. Revenge is going to be sweet, big guy. Tell Callie I love her." He clicked off his phone. "Sorry about that. We've got twins and my partner has a really touchy gag reflex."

Emmett nodded, dreaming of the day Amber's babies would be keeping him and his brothers up at night.

"Where was I before I started to sound like a lunatic?" Wright asked.

"About you and I getting in touch after I saw Sergei in the parking lot handing Juan the bag of drugs," Amber said.

"When did that happen?" Emmett asked.

Amber took his hand. "The day before you found me in the road.

I'm a therapist, or was a therapist, at a boys' home in Chicago. Juan was one of my boys. I saw Sergei, who was the director, hand him a bag of drugs one day. Juan is only twelve years old and a sweet boy. I had to act."

"Stone, your woman did act—and how. If you ever want to move to Bliss, there's a club that would certainly take you in as a member." Wright shook his head. "After taking the kid to her sister's house to make sure he was safe, she went against my instructions to stay away. She broke into Sergei's office and found drugs late one night with the intention of bringing them to me to help build a case against the creep."

"Wait just a second." Emmett fixed his stare on Amber. "Is this a habit of yours? To run headfirst into danger when told not to by people who know more than a little about such things?"

Her jaw dropped.

"I'll take that as a 'yes.' That's something we'll deal with later, pet." He turned back to Wright. "Go on, Sheriff. Finish the story."

"Sergei is…correction, was, the eldest son of the head of the Mitrofanov family, Niklaus. The Mitrofanovs lead a Russian syndicate based in Chicago. I have a friend back in Bliss who helped me map out the organization."

A syndicate? This was worse than Emmett could have imagined. "Are you telling me the Russian mafia are running the boys' home that Amber worked at?"

Wright nodded. "I am. Niklaus set the place up through regular channels. Times have been hard on charities, so fresh money is treasured in those circles. Along with some grants the place was awarded, he had a nice little operation that's been going for two years. The boys acted as transporters to and from the syndicate's main channels. The Mitrofanovs had to keep up appearances to the regulatory agencies that had jurisdiction over the property. Niklaus put Sergei in charge and some other underlings, but he had to have legit staff, too. Enter your Amber, or as I know her, Kathy. She was coming to Bliss, where I live, to hand over all the evidence she'd gotten her hands on. I was going to coordinate with the DEA and FBI. The minute my friend, Alexei, heard the name, he knew the mob was involved."

Emmett recalled the state she was in during the rainstorm. "'Bliss' and 'Wright' were the words you were saying when I found you, sweetheart."

"It's a twenty-hour drive from the boys' home to Bliss." Amber squeezed his hand. "I got lost somewhere before I got to Denver. Now that I've seen where Destiny is on a map, I must've headed west and north for a couple of hours. I had a flat tire and had to stop. I started walking and then the wind started blowing so hard. I tripped and fell."

"Baby, you should've followed Nate's advice."

Amber squeezed his hand. "If I had, I would've never met you, Emmett. You may not always like my impulsiveness, but I don't care what you say, I'm glad I tried to get to Bliss despite the risk."

"It was fate." Cody winked. "No doubt about it."

"What about the missing persons report from Chicago? It showed Amber as married."

Wright shook his head. "She's not. Apparently, the Mitrofanovs have a mole in that precinct. Not sure who, but I'll work with Sheriff Wolfe to see if we can figure it out. We're concentrating our investigation on Nicole Flowers, the officer who filed the report originally. Not sure if it was her, but someone there passed the information on to the Mitrofanovs when Wolfe contacted that office. Presto. Sergei and his goons show up. We'll figure out who leaked the information. Count on it."

"What about Sergei's father? What was his name?" Emmett asked.

"Niklaus Mitrofanov," Wright answered.

"Won't he come looking for Amber now that his son is dead?" At that very moment, Emmett wished he had his gun with him, his need to protect his woman growing with every beat of his heart. She'd done the noble thing to help Juan and the other boys, but that had put her on the radar of some very dangerous men.

"And you, too, Emmett," Wright said. "But Mr. Mitrofanov is being held by some friends of mine in the DEA."

"How long have I been out?" he asked.

"About eighteen hours," Bryant informed.

Mr. Mitrofanov would be a threat again soon. "Can't they only hold him for seventy-two hours without charging him?"

Wright smiled. "My buddies will find a way to hold him until we get everything in place that we need to charge him. You and your brothers left two of the Mitrofanov henchmen alive, though quite worse for the wear. They've already signed plea deals. With their confessions, the evidence Amber stashed in the home's van, and her and Juan's testimonies—Niklaus Mitrofanov will be locked up for the rest of his life." Wright grinned a little. "Which will very likely be a short one. Alexei assures me someone in prison will take care of the son of a bitch."

Emmett wasn't crazy about the idea of Amber having to testify, to show her face inside a courtroom. "How long before this goes to trial, Sheriff?"

Wright shook his head. "The wheels of justice move painfully slow, unfortunately. That's why it's always just best to shoot 'em. It's so much faster and with less paperwork. Oh, sure the doc will likely scream about having to do autopsies, but it's really easier in the end. I'd say eighteen months minimum, but Mitrofanov will be behind bars awaiting prosecution. He's a definite flight risk. The judge won't even set bail because of that."

Emmett knew how these things worked. There was always someone waiting to take over if the boss went down. "But there must be more to this syndicate family than Niklaus."

Amber sighed. "Nothing is going to happen to me or to you. You're worrying for nothing."

It wasn't "nothing." He couldn't lose her. "Look at me, Amber. In the eyes."

She obeyed, her eyelashes fluttering hypnotically.

God, how he loved her, but she could be headstrong and foolish. Bratty, too. "Time to set the record straight, sweetheart. I will never stop worrying about you, about your safety. That's my job. Now and forever, got it?"

She nodded, chewing on her lower lip like a good little sub.

"Better." Emmett turned back to Wright. "My question was about others in the crime family's employment."

"Unlikely," the sheriff said. "The Mitrofanovs' product has always been meth. The long-established Chicago mafia, The Outfit, has been in a turf war with them for quite some time. Add to that Sergei and the ten underlings you and your brothers took down, besides the two stool pigeons out of the picture, and any power the family has is gone. Keep your woman with you here in Destiny. Everything will be fine. I'll contact you with any new details that come up in this case. How's that agreement work for you, Emmett?" Wright held out his hand to seal the deal.

After Wright's account of where things sat, Emmett's strain of worry for his little one eased up. "Works fine, Sheriff." He shook the man's hand.

"Okay, that's it. I may not work in this hospital, but I am a nurse. One of you can stay, but everyone else out." Amber's sister was a real spitfire. "Emmett needs his rest."

Wright gave her a mock salute. "Stone, I'll be in touch."

"Better get back to your wife and kids." Emmett laughed. "Sounds like you and Zane have your hands full."

"Yes we do, and we're loving it, although I definitely need a new hat." Wright exited with a wave.

Belle nodded her approval. "That leaves five. I'm sure Juan is hungry, aren't you?"

"Yes, ma'am. May I have a hamburger?"

Amber's sister's edge softened as she looked at the boy. "Of course." She turned back to the rest of the group, and her inner hellcat, claws at the ready, was back. "Two more better be right behind us or else. The one who decides to stay better be quiet and let the patient go back to sleep. *Capisce?*"

Belle didn't wait for anyone to answer but turned with Juan and left the room.

"Your sister is something else, Amber," Cody said.

She smiled and shook her head. "Wait until you really get to know her."

Emmett looked at his brothers, his best friends in the world. "Don't think you're off the hook for your duties. The ranch can't run itself."

"You're right about that." Cody nodded, smiling. "I'm betting you'll milk the two itty-bitty bullets you took for several weeks."

"Two?"

Bryant nodded. "One in your chest and another in your leg, Emmett."

"Quite the overachiever," Cody teased.

In addition to the pain in his chest, he was suddenly aware of the soreness just above his right ankle. Pain meds must've been running low. "Are you saying that between the three of us we only have three good legs? Some kind of cowboys we make."

Emmett and his brothers laughed, though laughing for him was a few added twinges. Best to keep chuckles to a minimum for now.

"Sawyer and Reed are picking up the slack. Should they need help, Eric and Scott said they could come out."

Emmett smiled. The plane crash that took their parents also took Sawyer, Reed, and Erica Coleman's parents, as well as Eric and Scott Knight's. They'd all been teenagers at the time, and the event had sealed them together into a tight circle of eight orphans. "The Knight brothers might love being in the saddle more than being behind the desks at Two Black Knights, but I can't imagine they'll have time to check on our livestock and still run their multibillion-dollar company."

"TBK will be just fine." Cody's eyebrows shot up. "Hell, the thing practically runs itself now."

Amber squeezed Emmett's hand even tighter than before. "Master, I think you, Bryant, and Cody make the best kind of cowboys, working legs or not. I love you. I love all of you."

"I love you, little one." He turned to his brothers. "Get out of here before Broom Hilda returns. Amber stays. Deal?"

"You bet," Bryant said.

Cody nodded. "Take good care of our hero, sweetheart. We need him back on his feet."

"I promise, I will."

His brothers left him in the care of the woman who held their hearts in the palms of her delicate, little hands, the woman they would spend the rest of their lives with. "You and your sister are quite protective of Juan."

She nodded.

"You're going to be an amazing mother, Amber."

Seeing her sweet smile and pink cheeks was the best medicine in the whole wide world.

# Chapter Seventeen

Amber looked into the eyes of her completely healed cowboy Master, Emmett.

He, Cody, and Bryant were wearing their Dom attire—tight pants, leather harness, and military boots, all in black. Could there be a more mouthwatering trio? Her answer was an unequivocal "no."

She'd been sitting on the porch sipping tea when they suddenly appeared without warning in their sexy garb and commanded her into the playroom. Her body sizzled instantly that very moment. Emmett's recovery was over, and he was all the way back to his wicked, demanding normal.

"Time to strip our slave, brothers." Emmett cupped her chin. "You're going to be punished, pet."

His harsh stare made her a nervous wreck and made her body vibrate hotly. His recovery completed, his hunger seemed to fill the entire playroom.

"Color?" His word wasn't a gentle request. It was an order, an ultimatum, a mandate from her Master that best be answered or else, and it was the "else" that had her trembling.

"Green, Sir." She shivered just thinking about the pleasure to come. And the punishment? Reaching into her bravest parts, she risked her own question. "Master, what am I being punished for?"

"I've been planning this night, little one, since I woke up in the hospital and saw your sweet face gazing down at me."

That long? No wonder she couldn't tamp down her shivers. "You have, Sir?"

"Yes, I have. Cody and Bryant, your other Masters, have worked out the details with me."

They all looked so wonderfully wicked. Could she bear whatever it was they'd set up for her?

Emmett continued. "You remember what happened in the sheriff's office?"

"I did something wrong in there, Master?"

"Yes. I made it clear, and so did Bryant, that we wanted you to stay put. But you pushed back and batted those pretty eyelashes of yours. We're partly to blame, too, slave, but you should've obeyed us from the start. If you had, you would've been safe with us. I will not tolerate disobedience, little one. My job is to keep you safe, first and foremost. You kept me from doing my job. I don't want that to ever happen again."

Cody removed her top over her head. "Neither do I, sub." The flirty cowboy she'd first met in him was gone. His unsmiling face terrified and intrigued her.

Bryant removed her jeans. "We have to punish you."

Standing in only her bra and panties, she felt more exposed than ever, even though she'd been intimate with all of them. Cody and Bryant had introduced her to what a threesome could be like—too incredible for words. Emmett's tongue had ushered in new and overwhelming sensations she'd never known existed, and ever since, she'd been craving like mad to experience it again.

"You're our woman. Do you know what that means, little one?" Emmett asked.

From her head to her toes, she was theirs. "Yes, Sir."

"I'm not sure you do. But you will. You're our responsibility, slave. Ours to keep. Ours to protect. Ours to pleasure. Ours to do with as we please. Understand?"

"Yes, Master."

"You have to trust us. We know what's best for you. I'm glad you came to us, baby, but when I heard from Nate what led you to us, what you had done stealing those drugs, I about lost it." He turned to

Bryant. "Hand me Blackie."

Bryant nodded and handed the scary-looking black paddle to him—the same paddle Emmett had threatened her with the first time in the playroom. Then it had been a test. When he'd asked her color state, she'd confessed with "yellow." Now this wasn't a test. This was punishment, plain and simple. *Trust. I trust Emmett. I trust Cody. I trust Bryant.* She absolutely did trust her cowboys, but that wasn't backing down her nerves, not one bit.

Emmett swung it in front of her, and she felt the blast of air it moved on her face, giving her the worst case of the willies. "You're reckless and headstrong. Tonight you're going to learn what it means to disobey us. What happened in the past, back in Chicago, in the sheriff's office, can't happen again. We take the risks, not you. After tonight, you'll think twice before you act so rash."

He swung it again, and her heartbeats sped up in her chest and her breathing hitched tight in her throat.

What would the monstrous thing feel like on her ass? The other paddle had warmed her ass up quite nice. Would Blackie burn her until she couldn't stand on her own?

As Cody removed her bra and Bryant her panties, a palpitating shudder shot through Amber as her trepidation and wantonness came to blows, warring for supremacy inside her.

Bryant's lips feathered along her neck, raising her temperature several notches. "Time to get you on the bench, baby."

Her nipples and clit were tingling in anticipation as he and Cody tied her to the bench with ropes, real ropes.

"What your Masters, my brothers, are doing, little one, is trussing you to the bench so you can't move. We could've used handcuffs, but we want you completely immobile. Each of us carries two pairs of scissors in case you start to panic beyond the pleasurable state we want you in. Do you trust us, slave?"

"Yes, Master," she choked out, since getting enough oxygen in her lungs was becoming increasingly difficult. She was so turned on, and they'd only stripped away her clothes. God, she would never tire of their commands from their mouths, their hands, and yes, even their cocks. She could feel the bite of the ropes on all her flesh save one place, her bottom. The bites there would come from Blackie. She gulped, thinking about Emmett, who she could no longer see, standing behind her, staring at her ass, and holding the wicked punishing tool in his hand.

"I'm done with my knots," Cody informed in a deep, lusty tone.

Bryant brushed the hair out of her eyes, giving her a little dose of courage and a whole bunch of goose bumps. "Me, too. Our slave is ready for her punishment."

"How about a blindfold and ball gag?" Cody's suggestion heightened her tremors. "I know we didn't talk about using them, but I think our pet might get more out of the experience if we did."

"Good thinking," Emmett said. "But just the blindfold tonight. I want to hear her screams. Color, slave?"

Cody carefully covered her eyes.

"Green, Master." The truth was her green was vacillating in shades of worry and want. Still, she couldn't believe how easily she was settling into her cowboys' lifestyle. She was taking to BDSM play lickety-split. *Lick? God, please lick me again, Emmett.* She didn't dare say it out loud or anything else for that matter unless instructed to speak or answer. She didn't want Emmett to change his mind on the ball gag thingy Cody had mentioned.

"Let us train our slave, brothers." Emmett's voice was harsher than she'd ever heard it, sending butterflies aloft in her belly.

"You."

The first whack from Blackie in Emmett's hand to the very middle of her ass shocked a scream out of her, but she couldn't move even an inch with Cody's and Bryant's ropes around her. The sting continued to sizzle when he removed it from her backside.

"Will."

The next whack landed in the center of her left cheek. Blackie's chomp sizzled on her flesh, causing her nipples and clitoris to throb like mad.

"Obey." Her right cheek was scorched by the monstrous paddle's next attack, releasing a flood of tears from her eyes and pussy.

"You." *Thwack.* "Will." *Thwack.* "Obey." *Thwack.*

Over and over, Emmett said the same words, punctuating them with Blackie's teeth to her ass.

Never had she felt such overwhelming heat or mind-blowing dizziness. Every spank chipped away at her resistance, her hesitation, her walls, her doubts. The more the paddle landed on her now-molten ass, the more she surrendered herself to them. Trust. Absolute and total.

"Color?" Her Master's voice came through the delicious haze, filling her with rapture.

"Green, Master." Her own words seemed distant and faraway.

"Are you ready to obey us, little one? Always?"

"Yes, Masters. Always."

"Sweet surrender," Emmett said in a hushed tone that sounded like satisfaction to her.

"Beautiful," Bryant added in a similar timbre.

"She's ours. All ours," Cody said in a resonance matching his brothers'.

Their praise filled her with pride. She'd pleased her Masters.

"You're my everything, Amber." Cody's words reached into her and her heart swelled. She felt his lips on her forehead. "I love you, baby."

Before she could respond to him, another pair of hands caressed her. Bryant's deep tone vibrated along her skin. "You've changed me, sweetheart. I promise to spend the rest of my life making sure you know how much I love you." He kissed her cheek.

The passion in Bryant's voice filled her with joy. She parted her lips to confess how she felt about him, but then Emmett placed his hand gently over her mouth before she could.

"Wait, Amber. I have something to say first." He removed his hand but she remained silent as he wished. "I'd lost sight of what living was about. Since our parents' deaths, I did what I had to do to keep my brothers and me together. I don't regret a minute of it. We were brothers, yes, but all of us had forgotten what it meant to be a family. And then I found you in the road and everything changed." His words held a fierce devotion combined with a powerful tenderness that made her know she was really home. "You're my future. You're the love of my life, little one. I will never let you go, understand?" Emmett's lips crushed possessively into hers. Then he choked out a final word that shook her very soul. "Never."

Happy tears streamed down her face. Amber's amnesia had brought her to Destiny and to a new life, a life with her soldier cowboys—Emmett, Bryant, and Cody. This was blissful submission. They were hers as much as she was theirs. Through trembling lips, she whispered, "I love you, too."

In a flash, they removed the ropes and blindfold. She blinked her eyes, trying to adjust to the light as they all undressed.

"We're going to keep you on the bench, little one. Grab Bryant's hands. That's my girl. We're going to lower the bench so that we can all fuck you at the same time."

Her first thought, in her light-headed, lusty-filled state, was she had no idea the bench could be adjusted to a different height, and her second was how did they plan on fucking her simultaneously? As the contraption locked into the position her Masters wanted, her pussy got even wetter.

"Cody and I are going to slide you down the bench a few inches to give us better access to your pussy and ass," Emmett said in syllables clearly chock full of carnality.

They shifted her down.

She heard the sounds of condoms opening, and then Emmett lifted her up as if she were weightless. She saw Cody crawl onto the bench where she'd just been.

"I'm going to love feeling your pussy gripping my cock, pet." He growled with lust in his eyes. Her clit ached, driving her to the brink of maddening desire.

Emmett lowered her down onto Cody's body. She could feel his sheathed cock on her mound, making her even wetter. Then Emmett dribbled lube on her ass and began preparing it with his fingers, spreading them out inside her. She recalled how the plug had felt but knew his cock would stretch and fill her so much more.

"Now I want your sweet, little mouth." Bryant moved in close and lined up his cock to her mouth. "Enjoy your meal, pet."

She parted her lips, and her cowboy took immediate advantage. His hands grabbed the back of her head as he groaned and pushed his massive cock past her lips and down her throat. He tasted like man-candy, masculine and hot. She licked the pre-cum off the tip with her tongue, and hollowed out her cheeks, sucking hard on her cowboy's cock.

She tensed slightly as she felt Emmett's dick pressing against her anus.

"Let's claim our slave, brothers." Emmett's hot, howling tone ignited a fresh blaze inside her body.

Continuing to swallow Bryant's dick down her throat, she'd never known need to be so consuming, so unmanageable, so heavy. She wanted to be claimed by her cowboys, to have all their cocks inside her body.

Cody thrust his cock into her pussy, hitting her in that special place that burst her into flames, causing her clit to throb overwhelmingly and her pussy to clench tight around his shaft.

When she felt Emmett's cock deep inside her ass, she moaned into Bryant's cock. With each thrust in and out, he howled a single conquering word. "You. Are. Mine."

These three men loved her. They'd loved her when she didn't even know herself. They'd loved her when monsters came for her. They still loved her. She trusted them to love her forever. It was crazy and unbelievable how her life had changed. They'd rescued her and given her so much her heart could barely contain.

Completely vulnerable for their taking, she groaned at the feel of her Masters' big dicks in her mouth, her pussy, and her ass. Even without the ropes, she didn't have to move. Her cowboys were in charge, delivering waves of pleasure as they slid in and out in perfectly synchronized thrusts, plunging faster and deeper.

These were her Masters…hers…only hers. Her surrender was absolute and overwhelming. Her climax radiated from her womb, creating a tsunami of sensations that stretched and burned every nerve ending in her body.

Bryant moaned and held the back of her head. "Fuck, I'm coming. Swallow every drop, pet." His hot liquid hit her at the back of her throat, and she greedily gulped it all down.

Cody's cock drove into her hard and fast. "Here I come, baby. Damn." His last word trailed off into a manly moan of release. The spasms in her pussy clenched and unclenched on his dick, again and again.

Emmett's words of domination were muffled and husky. "You. Are. Mine." He thrust into her bottom over and over. Then she felt him buck up against her, sending his dick deep into her ass. She tightened her insides around him, enjoying the feel of his pulse inside her.

Her climax multiplied, pulsing faster and faster, hotter and hotter. She clung to the rhythmic sensations, riding out every sinful shudder. Frantic, wild pleasure shredded her to pieces, searing the pulse in her veins.

Bryant stepped back, slipping his sated cock from her mouth with a pop.

Without his cock to hold back her moans of ecstasy, they vibrated her lips violently as they escaped her throat. Trekking through a myriad of dizzy responses in her body, she closed her eyes tight, feeling tears stream from her eyes.

In a flash, she was off the bench and in Emmett's arms. He held her so tight to his chest she could actually feel his heartbeats on her flesh. Her pulse thudded through her body, a hot, humid throbbing. Bryant stroked her hair and Cody kissed her back.

"Open your eyes, little one." Emmett's tender command squeezed her heart perfectly.

She obeyed, and gazed into her Master's eyes.

"You will obey. Understand?"

"Yes, Master."

"And you will love us, too."

"Always."

* * * *

Amber sat in the booth at Blue's Diner with her three men. Emmett sat next to her and Cody and Bryant sat across from them. She still couldn't believe what they'd done for her, for her boys. But right in front of her on the table surrounded by four cups, three black coffees and her hot tea with cream and sugar, were architectural plans for a dormitory.

"This is amazing. You guys are serious about this?" she asked.

"We are," Bryant said.

"Hell yeah, we're serious," Cody added.

Emmett squeezed her hand. "We've got an appointment with Phoebe Blue today to update our wills and to get the paperwork started on donating a hundred acres to the new boys' ranch."

When she'd told them about all the boys at the orphanage and that they'd likely be shuffled like a deck of cards away from each other into foster homes, shelters, and other facilities, her guys had taken the reins and put this whole thing together in nothing flat.

Cody smiled. "Will you miss Chicago, baby?"

She shook her head. "My sister is here now. Juan, too, and soon all my other boys. I get to work as a counselor again, helping children. One trip back to my apartment to get my things and to end my lease should be all I need."

"How about we head up there next week?" Cody said, clearly eager to settle her into their houses—the one in town, which was a lovely ranch style on Big Elm Street behind the Dream Hotel, and their cabin on the ranch in the mountains, which she loved more than any other place in the world.

Two elderly, nice-looking gentlemen walked up to the booth.

The one with the white hair, red flannel shirt, and pipe spoke first. "How are you boys doing?"

"Just fine, Patrick," Emmett answered. "You and Sam haven't met Amber yet, have you?"

"No we haven't." He extended his hand to her.

"Nice to meet you two." She took Patrick's hand, and before she could stop him, he lifted the back of her hand up to his lips.

"And you."

"Forgive my brother, miss. He's a bit touched." The bald man with the white beard twirled a finger near the side of his head in the universal sign of crazy. "I'm Sam O'Leary. I thought Jason said your name is Kathy White."

"Legally it is. I've decided from now on to be called by the name these cowboys gave me when they found me—Amber."

"Nice to meet you, Amber." Sam held out his hand as Patrick had done.

"Likewise, Mr. O'Leary." She offered her hand to him, and like his brother, he also kissed the back of it.

Sawyer and Reed, the ranch hands and close friends of her guys, ran into the diner. The rugged mavericks wore their hair longer than most around Destiny, likely an outward sign of their inward rebellious natures. Sawyer had fierce green eyes, while Reed's were blue and inviting. "You guys are going to the courthouse, aren't you?"

"Of course they are," Patrick said. "The whole town will be there to watch my wife—"

"Our wife," Sam corrected.

"Our wonderful wife. She will be proceeding over the hearing."

"Ethel is a great judge," Bryant said.

"The greatest," the elderly men said in unison.

Amber had learned that the O'Learys had been like grandparents to her guys, the Knight brothers, and the Colemans—Sawyer, Reed, and their sister Erica—after all their parents had died in the plane crash together.

The diner was clearing out fast.

"We better hurry before all the good seats are taken," Patrick said.

He and Sam bolted out the door, followed by Sawyer and Reed.

"You guys were joking when you said Patrick actually believes in dragons, weren't you?" They'd mentioned it one day when they were telling her about the town. The man seemed quite reasonable and in his right mind to her.

Bryant smiled. "Just ask him yourself some day, but be ready to lose at least a couple of hours for his tirade on the subject."

Cody asked, "You've seen the statues around the park, baby?"

She nodded.

"Who do you think paid for them?"

"Patrick?"

"Yes. He's the richest man in town and maybe the most brilliant, too. So what if he believes in dragons? He might be right."

"Okay, we better head over to the courthouse now," Emmett said. "We don't want to miss all the fun."

* * * *

Emmett sat in the Swanson County Courthouse next to Amber, the woman he and his brothers would spend the rest of their lives with. He looked on the other side of the mahogany half wall dividing the courtroom in two. Eric and Scott stood next to Cameron Strange, TBK's corporate attorney. Behind them, in the gallery but just on the other side of the wall, was Cam's brother, Dylan, former CIA operative and head of security for Eric and Scott's tech company.

The normally rowdy citizens of Destiny were quiet, making it easy to hear across the courtroom.

"Look over there." Scott pointed at Emmett, Amber, and his brothers. "The playboys of Destiny have been tamed."

Eric frowned and hit his brother in the arm. "What the fuck do you mean by that? We're the reigning playboys. Always have been. Not the Stones."

Emmett smiled and waved at his good friends. Let them take the helm. They were excellent training Doms. Phase Four was now their domain. He wanted only one sub at his side, the love of his life, Amber.

"Shit." Eric waved back. He said something to Scott and Cam, but Emmett couldn't make it out.

Then Eric and Scott began checking out all the single women in the place. The billionaire brothers were sticking to their lusty routine. Once this was over, they'd most likely head straight to Phase Four for some fun.

Emmett had promised to take Amber to the club one day, but he and his brothers wanted to keep their play to the cabin for now. Once she was ready to be put on display, they'd gladly take her, proud to show off the love of their lives.

He grabbed Amber's hand. Bryant was sitting on the other side of her with his arm around her shoulders. Cody was just on the other side of Bryant, keeping his eyes on her alone, ignoring everyone else in the courtroom.

Life had changed for the better since he'd found Amber. No longer a "half-empty" kind of guy, he saw the world in a whole new light, and it all was because of her.

Suddenly, the back double doors flew open. All eyes turned to the new arrival. The woman Eric and Scott were suing for ten million dollars.

Megan Lunceford was an attractive young woman. He would guess her to be twenty-five or so. She crashed into Mitchell Wolfe, Jason's hellion brother, and a folder he was holding that held a ton of papers went flying in the aisle, spilling its contents in every direction.

"I'm so sorry," the woman said.

Scott's single word shocked him. "Wow."

Emmett turned and looked at him and Eric. What he saw on their faces shocked him. They were more than a little intrigued. They were captivated.

*Boys, you better watch out. The woman you're suing may very well turn your life upside down and sideways.*

Emmett leaned into Amber, the woman who'd done the exact same thing to him. "I love you, little one," he whispered.

# THE END

**WWW.CHLOELANG.COM**

# ABOUT THE AUTHOR

Chloe Lang began devouring romance novels during summers between college semesters as a respite to the rigors of her studies. Soon, her lifelong addiction was born, and to this day, she typically reads three or four books every week.

For years, the very shy Chloe tried her hand at writing romance stories, but shared them with no one. After many months of prodding by an author friend, Sophie Oak, she finally relented and let Sophie read one. As the prodding turned to gentle shoves, Chloe ultimately did submit something to Siren-BookStrand. The thrill of a life happened for her when she got the word that her book would be published.

***For all titles by Chloe Lang, please visit***
www.bookstrand.com/chloe-lang

**Siren Publishing, Inc.**
**www.SirenPublishing.com**

9 781627 400572